# A BAT AMONG BRUINS

## BROCK ENLOE

Published by Argyle Fox Publishing
argylefoxpublishing.com



ISBN 979-8-89124-084-1 (Paperback)
ISBN 979-8-89124-083-4 (Hardcover)
ISBN 979-8-89124-086-5 (Ebook)

*To my grandparents, John and Jeanette Enloe,*

*who now live in the stars. May this tale reach you.*

*Thank you for showing me the places that*

*inspired this made-up world.*

*I carry your sense of adventure and rich love*

*with me to this day. I love and miss you both!*

# A BAT AMONG BRUINS

# CHAPTER 1

# (1988) THE MOVE

John startled awake to the sound of his alarm clock screaming from his bedside table. He slammed his hand on the snooze button and buried his head under his pillow.

"Get up, Billy! Get up, John!" Mrs. Daggon entered the boys' bedroom and yanked the sheets off the boys. "It's moving day, and your father is waiting downstairs for you guys to help him load the truck."

"Oh, come on, Mom!" Billy reached for the sheet in his mother's hand. "It's not even seven!"

Mrs. Daggon rolled the two sheets into a single ball. "Well, we have a long drive ahead of us, and we need to get as far as we can today. That way, we have a shorter drive tomorrow." She unplugged the alarm clock and stuffed it inside the ball of sheets. "Your dad's boss recommended we get in before dark. Things don't stay open very long after sunset there."

"Ugh, why are we moving?" John asked from under his pillow. "I've never heard of this place, and it doesn't even have a beach."

"You know why we're moving," Mrs. Daggon said. "Your father got a great paying job working less hours. Now, get up—both of you! I won't tell you again!"

With that, Mrs. Daggon left the room, leaving Billy and John uncovered on their beds. The brothers yawned and wiped sleep from their eyes. Slowly, they sat up in their beds. They were moving, and they were moving today. No reason to prolong the inevitable.

Down the hall, their mother kept talking, expecting the boys to listen as she rambled. "Burdine, Missouri—you boys will love it there and make friends in no time. Plus, your dad and I heard their basketball team is struggling and could really use you guys."

The boys rolled their eyes at each other, then yanked on clothes and tennis shoes. They stumbled down the stairs to the living room. Mr. Daggon looked up.

"It's about time you boys got up and around." Mr. Daggon stood up and stretched his back. "Now help your old man with these last few boxes," he said with a wink.

John sighed. Billy grunted. They both grabbed boxes and pushed through the front door toward the moving truck parked on the street.

"Great way to spend the last few days of summer, eh?" Billy tossed a box inside the back of the truck and leaned against the bumper. "Packing up to move to some small hick town in Missouri. Think about it, we could've been on the beach right now."

John shook his head. "I know, I'm bummed too."

                    Brock Enloe

He heaved his box into the back of the truck. "But who knows, maybe this town won't be so bad."

"I guess we'll see."

Mrs. Daggon walked toward the truck, carrying a small box and a big smile. She handed the box to Billy, who set it on top of a stack of boxes inside the truck. Mr. Daggon locked the front door of their soon-to-be-former house, slammed the moving truck's rolling door shut, and off they went.

Mr. Daggon and Billy led the way in the moving truck, with Mrs. Daggon and John following closely behind in the station wagon.

John pushed the Bananarama cassette down into his tape player, popped the foam headphones on his ears, and leaned his head against the window. "Cruel Summer" filled his ears as they passed the beach. In the distance, a handful of kids were running and splashing in the waves. It was early for moving, but it was never too early—or too late—for the beach.

John turned in his seat to soak in the beach scene as long as possible. It got smaller and smaller, then disappeared altogether. John spun around and slouched in his seat until he drifted asleep.

After more than fifteen hours in the car, a handful of hours in a motel, and countless bathroom stops, Mrs. Daggon nudged John's shoulder. "Look!" she said. "I think we're finally here."

John sat up in his seat, wiped the slobber off his arm, and rubbed his eyes. His vision unblurred just in time to read the sign:

As Mrs. Daggon drove, John watched the sun begin to set behind the mountains. An old train bridge hung high above the fog and over the river below. John's eyes followed the river, which twisted through the trees until it vanished in the distance.

"Pretty view, right?" Mrs. Daggon said.

John gave an "Mm-hmm," his eyes fixed on the changing scenery.

Burdine High School sat on the outskirts of town. They passed it and kept moving toward the heart of town. John swiveled his head in time to see the town hall, movie theatre, and hardware store. Just before his mom turned off the main road, he spotted a barbershop and a drive-in diner.

A couple miles and a few turns later, Mrs. Daggon squealed with joy. "We're home!"

She guided the station wagon through an opening in a wooden fence. The sound of crunching gravel filled their ears. At last, John's eyes gazed upon an old farmhouse on a hill. It looked how he felt—bare and alone. A grassy field stretched behind the house to the tree line.

"So," John said sarcastically, "we live on a farm now?"

"No, silly." Mrs. Daggon pinched her son's leg playfully. "We don't have any animals."

Ahead of them, Billy flung open the door to the parked moving truck and hopped out. He scurried to the bushes that lined the front of the house and tilted his head back in relief.

     Brock Enloe

"There's your animal," John joked.

His mother started to scold Billy for peeing out in the open, but it was dusk, and no one was around. So, she put the car in park and laughed. She and John climbed out of the car and walked toward Mr. Daggon, who was unlocking the back door of the moving truck.

"John, check it out!" Billy ran toward them, zipping his pants. "Dad said our property goes all the way into the woods, that everything is ours until the railroad tracks. Let's go explore and check it out!"

"Not now, boys," Mr. Daggon said. "We have to unload first. It's almost dark, and my boss recommended we be settled in by then. Y'all can check it out first thing tomorrow morning."

"Come on, Dad—we can do that any—" Billy started.

"Listen to your father," Mrs. Daggon said.

Billy dropped his head. "Yes, ma'am."

Late that night, Billy scoffed. "A new house, but we still have to share a room? You've got to be kidding me."

John laughed and stared at the ceiling fan that rotated in calm, predictable circles. "Goodnight, bro."

***

The sun peeped through the window, and the smell of sizzling bacon floated through the bedroom door.

"Breakfast is ready," Mrs. Daggon called to Billy and John, who were already halfway down the stairs.

The boys were stuffing their faces with eggs, bacon, and biscuits as their dad walked in.

"Well boys," Mr. Daggon said, "looks like y'all get an extended summer. The school here doesn't start back for another three weeks."

"Thee mo' wees?" John said through a mouthful of biscuit.

"Yes, three more weeks," Mr. Daggon confirmed. "I went by the school this morning while I was in town and talked with the principal."

Billy leapt in the air and gave John a high-five. "Let's go!"

Mr. Daggon grinned. "I also got to speak with the basketball coach. He said to come by the school this week. They already had tryouts, but he'll put you guys through a workout and if things go well, he'll see about getting you on the team. Apparently, they struggled bad last year. I think he'll be happy to have you guys."

The boys agreed to swing by the school the next morning. Before they headed out, the doorbell rang.

"Oh, I totally forgot!" Mr. Daggon rubbed his chin. "Mr. Bardot, my boss, wanted to meet with me for an hour or so this morning to go over some work stuff. His son, Jimmy, is your age. Thought y'all could make a friend before school starts, so he brought him along. Just take him wherever you go. I'm sure it'll be fun!"

Billy swung an arm in mock excitement.

"Awesome!" John shook his head at Billy in disapproval.

An old guy and his son stood outside, mirror images of each other. The only difference was that the younger heavyset dude's brown, curly hair nearly reached to his shoulders. The older one had his brown curls cut short.

After awkward introductions, Mr. Daggon and his boss headed into the house. Billy, John, and Jimmy walked toward the tree line in silence. Eventually, John broke the ice.

"So, what grade are you in, Jimmy?" he asked.

He was a rising sophomore, same as John.

"Any hot chicks live here?" Billy asked.

Jimmy chuckled. "Uh, yeah dude. I mean, I think so."

"Well," Billy said, nudging John, "maybe this place won't be too bad after all."

John shrugged, then picked up a pine cone. "So, what is Burdine known for?" he asked. "What's there to do around here?"

Jimmy explained that Burdine isn't known for much. But they have the oldest train depot in the Frisco Railroad Company. The rail route stretches from way up north, straight through Burdine, all the way down into Memphis, Tennessee, and Birmingham, Alabama.

"Don't forget about the bat attacks!"

The boys turned to see a stranger running toward them.

"Who are you?" Billy asked.

"That would be your neighbor," Jimmy said.

The gangly stranger reached the group, and John realized his hair wasn't brown. It was dark red.

"Shane Huxley," the new boy said. He held out a hand for anyone to shake. No takers. He let it flop to his side. "Like Jimmy said, I'm your neighbor. My family owns Huxley Farms."

John tossed the pine cone at a squirrel that ran by.

"What ya doing here, Jimmy?" Shane asked.

"Dad brought me over to meet them"—Jimmy motioned toward Billy and John with his head—"while our dads talk work."

Billy took a step toward the woods. The other boys followed his lead.

"Wait a second." Billy paused in mid-step and raised a hand in the air. "You said something about bat attacks. What's that all about?"

Shane flapped his arms in the air. "Yeah, man—the mountain bats! They attacked and killed some people in the forties or something."

Billy's eyes bulged.

Jimmy kicked at a pine cone. "Yeah, he ain't lying. There were a series of bat attacks back in the day. At least that's what everyone says."

Shane said that according to his dad, that was why the town pretty much closes at dark. It also explained why the Frisco Railroad workers make such big money. The train went over the bridge and through the cave in the mountain, where the famed bats lived. Shane pointed to the train bridge sitting high between the mountains in the distance.

"Oh, whatever dude!" Jimmy shoved Shane. "They don't even use that track route anymore. My dad said they boarded up the cave entrance and changed the route."

Shane held up his hands. "If I'm wrong, then why'd they board up the entrance and close that railroad?"

"Probably because the cave collapsed," Jimmy said.

Shane didn't respond. Just shoved his hands in his pockets and squinted at the bridge.

                    Brock Enloe

"Okay, well..." John shook his head, trying to put his thoughts in order. "Then why does the town close at dark then?"

"Simple," Jimmy said. "There ain't nothing to do here in the day time. Even less after dark."

"Deny all you want, but you know it's because of the mountain bats. That's why people don't like going outside after dark. It's also why downtown Burdine has them bright, humming street lights. They think that will repel the bats," Shane said, "but most people just don't stay out after dark anyway."

"Don't listen to Shane," Jimmy said. "Hasn't been a bat attack in years."

"That we know of," Shane murmured.

The boys stood at the edge of the tree line. Then John stepped forward and led the way into the thick of the woods. The foursome weaved between towering trees and hanging limbs, jumped a small creek, and wound through boulders scattered throughout the forest.

The shrubbery and woods grew denser. They trekked on until it was nearly impossible to move ahead. Just when John was ready to turn back toward home, he pushed his way into a small opening. In the middle of the opening, completely surrounded by dense forest, was a weathered wooden barn. The siding was practically fossilized, but the structure stood firm and upright. Here and there, a few planks were bowed back by age. Some dangled by a single rusty nail. But there was no opening large enough to give a clear view of the inside.

The boys made their way to the front, where the antique glass door was remarkably intact, though a little fogged up with dirt and moss.

John reached out toward the door. "Here goes nothing." He twisted the frail brass door knob, and the door groaned open slowly.

One by one, they stepped inside. Jimmy pointed at railroad tracks that covered the floor, stretching all the way to the opposite barn door. Then he began to walk across them, testing each step to make sure the ground was solid.

John climbed a ladder to inspect the barn's loft. There was no hay or pitchfork. Rather, there was an old bed, a bedside table with an antique lantern, and a wooden desk with several drawers. John opened the drawers, not sure what he hoped or feared to find.

Below, Jimmy reached the opposite barn door and removed the wooden plank keeping the door closed. The doors swung wide open and light poured in.

Billy and Shane gasped.

"No way!"

John slammed the desk's top drawer closed and rushed down the ladder to see what the stir was about. In the back corner of the barn, Billy and Shane pulled a sheet off a large, mysterious object. As the sheet fell, an old Frisco Railroad Company handcar revealed itself.

This wasn't a random barn. It was a historic Frisco depot cabin.

"Alright, this is definitely the hangout spot!" John exclaimed. The boys nodded their heads in agreement. "It could use a little work," he added, "but we can fix this up in no time."

"I got nothing to do," Billy said. "Let's start today!"



Brock Enloe

"Nah." Shane knocked on the handcar. "A bunch of kids from school are throwing a party on the lake today."

Jimmy slapped his leg, making a tiny dust cloud. "I totally forgot about that," he said, "but I'm down to go."

"Alright, well that's it. We'll all go," Shane said. "Y'all ride with me, and we'll go on my boat. It's a piece of junk, but it floats. Usually."

Jimmy suggested they begin work on the barn the next morning. Shane liked the idea, but Billy and John couldn't make it. Basketball tryouts came first.

"Y'all play basketball?" Shane smirked at Jimmy.

John tapped his foot on the barn floor and crossed his arms. "Yeah, what's so funny about that?"

"Well," Jimmy said with a laugh, "the basketball team here—well, they suck. Bad. Like, they hardly ever win a game."

"We heard as much," Billy admitted.

Jimmy and Billy pulled the double barn doors closed and dropped the plank back into place to keep it closed. They exited the front door and headed back toward the house.

Shane promised to pick them up at one, then jumped the fence and took off for his house.

"You boys have fun?" Mrs. Daggon asked as John, Billy, and Jimmy entered the kitchen.

"Is it okay if we hit the lake with Shane and Jimmy?" Billy opened a sleeve of saltines and slid a whole one in his mouth. He broke it in two and put half in each cheek. "Shane's coming to get us at one. A bunch of kids from school are having a lake party."

Mrs. Daggon looked at Mr. Daggon and Mr. Bardot.

"Just try to get your boxes unpacked before you leave."

Mr. Bardot motioned for Jimmy that it was time to leave. The two moved toward the front door, and Mr. Bardot called over his shoulder, "You guys just be home by dark!"

John and Billy spent the next few hours unpacking. A few minutes after one, the doorbell rang, and off they went without as much as a goodbye.

As the boys put the boat in the water, Jimmy screwed up his face. "You sure this thing runs, bro?"

They all laughed and hopped in. Shane turned the key in the ignition, and the motor coughed to life. They began slowly making their way across the waves.

"Dude," Billy said, "this thing goes like ten miles per hour!"

"I didn't say it goes fast." Shane patted the steering wheel with affection. "I said it floats."

John tilted his head back as the ten-mile-per-hour wind blew his blonde curly hair back. He asked where they were headed.

"Goat Island!" Shane shouted, pointing to a huge cliff in the distance.

As they puttered toward their destination, John kept his eyes on the big iron bridge floating in the mountain, remembering the story Shane told earlier that day. Were there really killer mountain bats? And if so, what happened to them?

Eventually, the boat made it across the lake. Shane killed the sputtering engine and let the boat coast to a stop at the base of the sixty-foot cliff. Jimmy leapt to the bow of the boat and tied it off on a tree branch.

"Where is everyone?" Billy asked.

Shane and Jimmy craned their necks to look up at the cliff, nonchalantly answering Billy's question.

John held a hand over his eyes to shield against the sun. "How do we get up there?"

"Gotta climb!" Shane jumped into the water and swam the short distance to the base of the cliff. "Come on, follow me!"

Soon, the foursome made their way to the top. As they reached the summit and pulled themselves onto flat ground, a crowd greeted them.

"Yo!" someone yelled. "It's Shane and Jimmy!"

John and Billy followed behind.

"Hey, everybody!" Shane flailed his arms in the air to get the crowd's attention. "This is John and Billy Daggon—they just moved here. Billy is a junior, and John is a sophomore."

The brothers waved and nodded. A couple people came up and introduced themselves before the boys settled down under a tree. From their under-the-tree seats, they listened to all the conversations taking place. Some talked about school, others talked about the latest movie sensation—*Die Hard*, and a few went on about some local murder that took place a year prior.

John tried to tune in to the murder talk. He wondered what it was all about and whether it had anything to do with bats. But a girl walked up and introduced herself to the new arrivals.

"I'm Rachel." Her voice was soft. She smiled at Billy and shook his hand. Her hand was soft too. John sensed a vibe between her and Billy.

"Yeah, yeah, we know who you are." Shane took her hand and shook it dramatically. "Just say what you want, that you want to get to know Billy."

Rachel blushed and asked Billy if he wanted to see the other side of the island

"Uh, yeah," Billy said. "Sure." He took Rachel's extended hand and walked off with her.

John watched them walk away as newcomers climbed over the clifftop. Then he saw her for the first time.

Her tan legs stretched the tensile strength of her faded blue jean shorts, and her brown curly hair blew in the wind. After scanning the growing group of partygoers, she locked her deep blue eyes with John. She gave him a warm smile.

John swallowed hard. "Who is that!"

"That is Cassie Mentz." Jimmy clucked his tongue. "A junior at Burdine."

"Out of your league is what she is," Shane added.

"Yeah, man. I'm not trying to side with Shane," Jimmy said, "but she's turned down every dude who has asked her out. Like, every dude."

The boys gawked at her. She returned the favor, and they quickly looked away, hoping she didn't notice. An awkward moment passed. Then—

"Aye, new kid—everyone here has jumped off the cliff. It's your turn to earn your place on the island!"

John didn't see who stated the challenge, but everyone heard it. He looked to Jimmy and Shane for help.

"He's lying. No one has ever jumped." Shane exhaled loudly. "Eric's just trying to get you to jump. He's a douche, just ignore him."

                    Brock Enloe

John relaxed, but only for a moment. Eric the douche was stomping through the crowd, leading a one-word chant: "Jump! Jump! Jump!"

Shane shook his head in disbelief, as a sizable crowd joined in the chorus and approached John. With everyone looking at him, John stood up and brushed off his hands and the back of his shorts. Shane and Jimmy eyed John, pleading him in silence to sit down.

John walked to the edge of the cliff and looked down at the water. A sudden dizziness struck him. He backed away from the edge and turned to the crowd. He pinched his eyes shut and took a couple deep breaths. The world stopped spinning, and he felt stable on his feet.

"He's scared," Eric shouted. "He ain't gonna jump!"

The crowd of high schoolers laughed. John didn't know any of them, and this was his warm welcome. Eric restarted his chant. Others joined in. John realized the basketball team wasn't the only thing that sucked in Burdine.

The chant grew. John turned his back and faced the cliff again. He took a resolute step forward, then another. He clenched his fists twice, then put his right foot behind him.

Just as he pushed off his back foot, someone grabbed his arm.

"Bro!" Billy practically screamed at his brother. "Screw this dude. You got nothing to prove to these people. Remember, we got to try out for basketball tomorrow."

John flexed against Billy's hold.

"Aw, how cute," Eric said in a baby voice. "His older brother is here to protect him. That's just so sweet!"

Shane held his head in embarrassment. Jimmy mouthed, "Do not jump," over and over. Cassie, the out-of-John's-league cutie, halfheartedly joined the chant encouraging John to jump. A bird flew overhead and cawed.

"Let go of my arm, Billy." John gritted his teeth.

Billy slowly eased his hold on John.

"I'll be right back." John flashed a little grin at Eric, darted toward the edge of the cliff, and jumped.

The chanting stopped immediately. For a moment, no one moved. Then the whole group moved like a herd to the cliff.

Meanwhile, John was falling, falling, falling. He regretted his decision and wondered if the falling would ever end. And then—*SPLASH!*

He cut through the water, and waves splashed and rippled over his head. He was still under when the surface of the water calmed.

Billy stared into the dark blue water, frantically searching for his brother to rise to the surface. But John didn't show. Time moved in slow motion. The crowd's excitement transitioned to palpable fear. Billy readied himself to jump, to search for his lost brother.

*Sphhht!* John broke through the surface, spewing water and gasping for air. He shook his head wildly, sending water spraying from his curly hair.

The crowd cheered and began a new chant: "John! John! John!"

Billy rubbed his hands together as Shane and Jimmy slapped him on the shoulder.

"He did it!" Jimmy said. "And he's okay."

     Brock Enloe

John smiled up at his brother and turned to see Cassie smiling big and wiping imaginary sweat from her forehead. Maybe she wasn't that far out of his league.

When John made his way back up the cliff, he sat down with Shane, Jimmy, Billy, and Rachel.

"Bro," Billy said, "don't scare me like that, dude!"

The group cracked jokes, insisting John was the dumbest and bravest and luckiest of them all. Jimmy looked at his watch and pushed himself to his feet. The day was nearly over. They should get back before sunset, especially since they were in Shane's beater of a boat.

Billy gave Rachel a final smile and said he'd see her around soon. John peeked at Cassie, who was eyeing him. He turned away embarrassed and confused and walked after Shane, Jimmy, and Billy who already started climbing down the cliff.

On the boat trip back to shore, the boys hooted and hollered.

"You weren't lying about hot chicks, Jimmy!" Billy said. "Y'all got 'em here, for sure."

"Yeah dude, you were spot on!" John laughed. "And I know y'all saw Cassie check me out as we were leaving."

"Yeah, she was looking at you," Shane said, "and she was thinking, 'There goes that idiot who jumped off Goat Island.'"

"You're just jealous." John puffed his chest out in a superhero pose.

Jimmy asked Billy what was going on with him and Rachel.

"She's cool," Billy said. "We just walked around and talked."

"Yeah…" Shane stretched the word out until it nearly broke. "You just walked and talked. I'm sure you're telling the truth, the whole truth, and nothing but the truth."

At the boat ramp, the boys loaded up and strapped the boat down to the trailer. John applauded Shane for telling the truth about his boat. "It did indeed float," he said. "It didn't do much else, but it stayed above the waterline."

Shane laughed as the crew piled into his truck. A few minutes later, he came to a dusty stop in the Daggons' gravel driveway. Jimmy hopped out and ran to his car. "Good luck at tryouts," he hollered back at John and Billy. "See y'all tomorrow!"

John turned to Billy as Jimmy's car and Shane's truck cruised down the Daggons' driveway. "Told you this place wasn't so bad," he said.

Billy threw an arm around his little brother and agreed.

Laying on his bed, John pulled out his journal. His grandma used to write in hers every night. When John asked her why, she said, "I write to relive the moments that have built the person I am today." It sounded like a good reason, so John started writing in his own journal.

The entry ran like a timeline for the last couple days. John wrote about the move to Burdine and his first friends, Jimmy Bardot and Shane Huxley. *Jimmy is a pretty funny dude*, John wrote. *His laugh is very high pitch, that alone will make you laugh.* Shane was labeled a *pretty cool dude.*

The journal entry went on to cover the discovery of the old train depot, the rumor of past bat attacks, and

 Brock Enloe

the party on Goat Island. He wrote briefly about Billy and Rachel and his leap of faith off of Goat Island, then focused where his brain had been all evening: Cassie.

> She is such a babe! I'm talking smokin hot, brown curly hair, deep blue eyes, the prettiest smile, tan legs, and curves in all the right places.
> The boys said I have no shot with Cassie... they said that she has turned down everyone who has asked her out. But we locked eyes several times today. It could be me overthinking but I am going to say she was looking at me.
> Haven't spoke a word to her yet...

"Dude, turn the light off and go to bed." Billy rolled over dramatically. "We got tryouts in the morning!"

"Alright. Alright." John scribbled a final line—*but it will happen!*—before he put his journal away and switched off the lamp.

***

"Boys!" Mr. Daggon stood in the doorframe of John and Billy's bedroom. "I've been yelling at you for five minutes. Get up! I'm dropping you off at Burdine High on my way into town!"

Fifteen minutes later, the brothers were pushing their way out the door. Each had a bagel in one hand and a half-drank, lidded Tupperware cup of orange juice in the other.

Mr. Daggon grabbed the car keys. "Got your basketball shoes?"

The boys assured him they did and filed into the station wagon.

On the short drive to school, Mr. Daggon reminded his sons to work hard, do their best, and not worry. "You guys could make any team you try out for," he said, "especially this one. Y'all will do great!"

"Thanks, Dad." Billy wiped orange juice from his mouth.

The station wagon slowed down. Mr. Daggon put the car in park as his sons climbed out. "I'll be back in an hour," he said. "Got to run a few errands! Good luck!"

Billy thanked his dad as he swung his arms in circles and jogged in place. John crossed his arms and bit the bottom of his lip.

"Breathe, little brother," Billy said as they walked toward the gym. "We got this. No need to be nervous."

Over the doors, big hand-painted letters read, THE DEN: Home of the Burdine Bruins.

"That is sick." John nodded in approval of the sign.

The gym was a typical high school gym. With the typical high school smells.

"You boys must be the Daggon brothers." A pale, balding man studied the two boys. Besides Billy and John, he was the only other guy in the gym. He reached a hand out just beyond his belly. "I'm Coach Jenkins."

Billy shook Coach's hand. "Billy Daggon," he said. "And this is my little brother, John Daggon."

"As you know, we already had tryouts," Coach said, shaking John's hand vigorously, "but we could use the help. So, if y'all impress me, I'll give you a jersey today along with practice and game schedules. Sound fair?"

        Brock Enloe

"Yes, sir," John said.

Coach raised an eyebrow at Billy.

Billy pulled his right arm across his chest to stretch. "Yes, sir."

Over the next hour, Coach Jenkins put them through an intense workout—dribble drills, defensive slides, shooting spots, passing, and a conditioning test well beyond the limits of what most terrible teams require.

By the time Coach blew his whistle to signal the end of the workout, John and Billy were drenched in sweat. The coach dabbed his own face with a clean towel. "I gotta be honest," Coach said. "I could have ended this workout ten minutes after it started. I need you guys, and you're good."

Billy doubled over with his hands on his knees. "Thank you, coach," he said, trying to catch his breath.

Coach motioned for the Daggon brothers to follow him, then walked through the locker room and into his office. He asked about basketball at the Daggons' old school in North Carolina. Billy explained that the team made the Elite Eight last season. He was the team's starting shooting guard, and John was the sixth man, a point guard.

"Wow!" The coach chuckled and rubbed his belly. "Well, you ain't going to be a sixth man here."

John's heart skipped a beat. He was going to sit the bench? Wasn't the team terrible?

"The seniors won't be fond of it," Coach said, "but you boys are my starting point guard and shooting guard."

John's heart returned to its normal rhythm as Coach threw a jersey at him. He unfolded the baby blue jersey outlined with white trim. The number three rested underneath Burdine spelled in all caps.

Billy held his number seven jersey out for inspection.

"Thanks, Coach! The numbers are spot on," John said. "Wrong shade of blue though."

"Oh no," Coach groaned. "Don't tell me you boys are Duke fans."

"Yes, sir, the biggest," Billy said. "But in all seriousness, these jerseys are perfect. Thanks again, Coach."

Coach handed them schedules and told them practice started the first day of school. "You boys enjoy the last few weeks of summer, and I will see you soon."

On the ride home, Mr. Daggon asked about tryouts.

"We made the team," Billy said excitingly.

"We're both starters!" John held out his jersey.

"I told you guys you would be fine," Mr. Daggon said, "but that's the wrong shade of blue."

"That's what we said," John laughed.

Mr. Daggon turned up the radio and drove right past the turn to their street.

"Dad?" Billy said.

Mr. Daggon held up a finger. "I've got one more errand to run, and then we're headed home."

Lo-fi oldies sang through the station wagon speakers as Mr. Daggon turned into a random driveway. A small brick rancher sat behind a row of well-kept hedges. A tabby cat ran to the backyard and out of view, behind a detached garage.

"Dad?" John looked at Billy in confusion. "Where are we?"

Mr. Daggon told his boys to get out of the car and

lend a hand. The boys stepped out of the car, unsure what they were helping their dad do.

Before they could ask, the door of the detached garage opened. An old lady wearing pink curlers and a pink bathrobe walked through the open door like she owned the place. Mr. Daggon greeted her and dropped three one-hundred-dollar bills into her hand. She handed him a set of keys.

Billy scratched his head.

"I figured y'all would need a set of wheels to get to school, practice, and work," Mr. Daggon explained. "Well, when you get a job. So, anyway—here is your hot rod." He tossed Billy the keys and pointed toward the garage.

Billy's jaw dropped. He smiled at the old lady and walked into the garage alone. When he came back out, he was in his new ride, a 1971 Green Plymouth Fury III.

John skipped to the car and hopped into the passenger seat. He cranked the passenger window down and slapped the outside of the car. "Let's roll!

"Thanks Dad! This is awesome!" Billy revved the engine. "Sorry, ma'am."

The elderly lady waved off Billy's apology. "Just be careful."

"Yes, ma'am," Billy said.

"Gotta admit," John said, "this is very cool, Dad!"

Following his dad home, Billy patted the steering wheel roughly. "I'm hype we have a ride, but dude, this thing is ugly!"

"Man, don't say that. She can hear you!" John rubbed the dashboard gently.

"So, what are we gonna call her?"

The two sat with the question for the rest of the ride home. In the driveway, Billy slammed on the brakes and spun the wheel, sliding into an opening beside the station wagon.

John got out in a cloud of dust. Coughing, he stepped away from the car and gave it another look. "I've got her name," John said. "The Fury."

"Oh, dude," Billy said, "that's it."

Soon as the boys showered and ate lunch, the doorbell rang. John shoved the last bite of food in his mouth and dropped his plate in the sink on the way to the front door.

"Y'all ready?" Shane asked.

Billy and John yelled into the house that they were heading out and stepped on the front porch.

"So, you guys make the team?" Jimmy asked as they started toward the depot.

"Yeah, man." John shot an imaginary basketball into an imaginary basketball goal. "Practice starts in three weeks."

At the depot, the boys wasted no time starting Project Clean-up. John swept the wooden floors, both upstairs and downstairs. Jimmy wiped the whole place down and cleaned the dirt-fogged window on the front door. Billy and Shane moved boxes and other random items around to make the space feel open and homey. At least it was homey for high school guys.

Billy swiped his hand across his forehead and flung sweat against the wooden floor. "It's clean, but we need a couch or something. Unless we plan to sit on the floor."

Shane asked Jimmy if they could use some of his grandpa's old stuff. Jimmy thought a moment. Some of his grandpa's furniture was in storage and collecting dust. May as well put it to use. Then Billy wondered how they would get furniture all the way to the depot. It was a hike, and the thick brush wouldn't make it any easier.

"What if we used the handcar," John suggested. "You know, wheel it here on the tracks."

"That's crazy talk," Billy said.

"Wait a second!" Shane rummaged through an open box and grabbed a large, creased piece of paper out of it. He slammed it on top of another box. "Saw this earlier. It's a map."

Jimmy, John, and Billy gathered around. According to the yellowed map, old railroad track ran straight through Burdine and passed behind the storage unit where Jimmy's grandpa stored extra furniture. It was almost too easy. As if someone or something wanted to make the transfer as simple as possible.

"Alright, that's the move then." John walked to the handcar. "Jimmy and I will take this to the storage unit and grab what we can."

The other two headed to the Daggon house to grab some sheets for the twin bed in the loft. They were also supposed to get a radio if they could or some other form of entertainment, so they would have something to do while they hung out.

John and Jimmy heaved the handcar onto the tracks, slid the wheels in place, and hopped on. The car glided along the rails, curving through the backside of the forest and over a small wooden bridge that hid the creek below.

Then the track reached a junction.

"Right or left?" John said.

"Hang a left. That'll take us through town." Jimmy pulled out the map for a confirming glance. "If we stayed on past town, it would run us all the way up to the iron bridge and into the mountain. But"—Jimmy pulled the map within inches of his face—"then the map stops there for some reason." He folded the map and slipped it back in his pocket.

"Left it is," John said.

John and Jimmy guided the cart left and rode along the outskirts of town. John recognized the drive-in diner and other buildings he passed when he first arrived to town. They nearly passed through the entire town before Jimmy pointed at a building. An overhead sign claimed the building was home to the World's Best Storage. John didn't realize there was so much competition.

"Here we are," Jimmy said. He walked down the line of slide-up doors until he reached the third from the last. He stuck a key in the lock and slid the storage door.

Dust danced in the air as the sun lit the inside of the storage unit. Jimmy and John were immediately drawn to the big couch. It was in decent-enough shape to sit in a barn, and it didn't smell. They lifted it and maneuvered it onto the handcar. It fit, and there was a little more room.

"Let's see what else we can find," Jimmy suggested.

The boys crawled into the storage unit and scavenged for anything that might be useful in the depot. John pawed a dartboard and darts and passed them to Jimmy.

"Sweet!" Jimmy placed the set on the ground outside of the storage room. He looked down the row of storage units to the rail cart, where the couch tottered in place.

"Jimmy! Dude, you didn't tell me your granddad was a Pirate!"

"Huh?" Jimmy turned back to the storage building, where John waved a pirate flag overhead. "He wasn't, you idiot. We got that on vacation in Florida."

"Oh well. It'd been cooler if he was a pirate, don't you—"

"Yeah, whatever dude." Jimmy shook his head and climbed to the back of the unit, where John was. "What else is back here?"

John tossed a bag of clothing aside, revealing a box labeled WWII.

"Grab that," Jimmy said. "I didn't know it was in here."

John groaned as he bent down to pick up the box. He waddled out of the storage unit and dropped it to the ground with a heavy thud. Jimmy kicked the box gently. "My granddad was a paratrooper. Jumped into Normandy in 1944."

"Pirate would've been cooler," John said, "but a soldier is pretty cool too, I guess."

Jimmy laughed and closed the storage room door. Together, they carried the WWII box and strapped it to the handcar. And off they went, back toward the depot, carting a random selection of items pilfered from Jimmy's grandad.

Billy and Shane eagerly greeted Jimmy and John. They helped drag the cart back inside the depot, then began inspecting the loot. The foursome spent the rest of the afternoon decorating and arranging the depot until they got it just right.

"Looks good to me!" Shane said.

"Not so fast," Jimmy said. "It needs one last touch." He pulled out the pirate flag and nailed it to the wall.

"Why the pirate flag?" Billy questioned.

"Why *not* the pirate flag?" John said. "That's the real question."

Three of the boys posted up on the couch, while John sat on the floor of the loft, dangling his feet over the edge.

"So, what are we gonna call it?" John asked.

"Call what?" Shane responded.

"This place," John said, "our hangout."

"We've got a pirate flag in here," Billy said. "What is a cool piratey name?"

"Argh, matey!" Shane yelled with his best pirate accent. "What say ye to The Roost?"

"The Roost?" Jimmy asked.

"Yeah, like the crow's nest on a pirate ship." Shane cleared his throat and continued in his normal voice. "So, you know, we keep the bird terminology going and just change the species of bird. The Roost."

John stifled a laugh. "I mean, it does have a ring to it."

"It's settled then," Billy said. "It's The Roost."

          Brock Enloe

# CHAPTER 2

# BACK TO SCHOOL

In the three weeks leading up to school, Billy put a lot of miles on his '71 Fury. He and Shane took it regularly to the dam outside of town to hang out with juniors and seniors from Burdine High. The weekend *Rambo III* opened, he let John get behind the wheel and drive the whole crew—John, Billy, Jimmy, and Shane to the theater. John figured Billy let him drive so Rachel Pierce wouldn't see him driving that ugly beater. She worked at the theater and hooked them up with free popcorn every time they went.

While John didn't get to drive much, he didn't mind. He and Jimmy spent their time fixing the old handcar. They spray-painted it black, attached a light to the front, and made it where they could sit down and pedal instead of having to stand and pump. They even attached a small motor. Granted, it doesn't provide any speed, but it helps with incline.

Most evenings were spent at The Roost. The boys threw darts, talked about girls, and listened to Cardinals games on the radio. A month ago, John and Billy had no interest in the St. Louis Cardinals, but now it was their team. These nights usually ended with Shane telling some sort of scary story as the whole crew sat around wide-eyed.

John journaled about it all, including how he wasn't sure what to make of Shane's stories.

> Most of the stories he tells are made up I think, but he did tell the story of the murder that happened last year. Some dude went on a killing spree and while running from the police he wandered through this area and shot someone in cold blood. Execution style he claims. Jimmy usually doesn't put too much weight into Shane's stories but he did say this one was a real deal. And I remember the people at the lake talking about a murder last year too.

One night, the boys built a bonfire pit, but before the fire really got going, a loud screech rang through the woods. It gave everyone the heebie-jeebies, especially Jimmy. He didn't like being out after dark anyway. Hearing that sound confirmed Shane's mountain bat theory—in Jimmy's head, at least. So, they tossed dirt over the fire to snuff it out and hadn't tried another fire since.

During the last week of summer, John and Jimmy took the handcar up the mountain past the state park to fish in the river. Jimmy taught John to fly fish, and they

　　　　Brock Enloe

caught a lot of rainbow trout and an occasional brown. It took about twenty-five minutes to get there from The Roost, but the ride on the handcar made the trip fly by. They passed through the outskirts of town, then rolled through a canopy of pines and firs on the old tracks, with the river rushing and trickling over the rocks, until they eventually came to a stop on top of the mountain, where they gazed down at the small town below.

They always stopped shy of the iron bridge, but that changed on the last day of summer. Billy was going to join, but Rachel invited him and Shane to the lake with her and another girl. So, they abandoned the railcar for a double date and promised to meet up with Jimmy and John at the drive-in diner that night.

John finished writing about the upcoming trip as footsteps sounded in The Roost.

"Yo, you up there?" Jimmy shouted at the loft.

John slid his journal in the desk drawer and started down the ladder.

"So," Jimmy said, "the iron bridge today?"

John grinned and began to push the handcar out of The Roost. Half an hour later, they reached their destination.

"Dude!" John yanked on the handcar brake when they reached the middle of the bridge. "Look at that view!"

"You can see everything, man," Jimmy whispered.

Down below, the sun reflected off the lake. In the opposite direction, the high school was an unimpressive rectangle awaiting the excitement of the coming days. The crisp mountain air was the perfect complement to the view, and Jimmy and John soaked them both in, doing their best to stretch out every minute remaining of summer vacation.

A squirrel chattered in a treetop just below the bridge, then leapt onto the tracks. The little guy gained his footing and skittered away.

"Let's go that way," John said. "We can see the entrance to the mountain. The map says it's just around the corner."

Jimmy leaned back and put his hands behind his head. "No reason to see it, it's just a boarded-up hole."

"Maybe, but I still want to see it." John released the brake, and the boys crept across the bridge and around the corner. The map was right. The entrance was right there. Jimmy was right, too. It was a boarded-up hole.

"I told you," Jimmy said. "Can we go now?"

John tilted his head, then yanked on the brake. He hopped off the railcar and walked the tracks toward the closed entrance. STAY OUT was spray-painted in red on the barricade. John banged on the wooden barrier.

"Come on—I'm hungry dude." Jimmy spun on the railcar and looked behind him. "We got to meet Billy and Shane at the diner soon, and we got a long trip down to get there."

"Okay, okay." John leaned toward the barricade and peeked through a crack. "Just give me one minute." There was nothing to see but darkness. The kind of darkness you can't penetrate. Cool wind from the depths of the mountain caves blew through the crack.

"Come on, dude."

John pushed away from the cave. As he did, something

        Brock Enloe

caught his eye—a shadow, a big shadow that was darker than the darkness in the cave moved across his field of vision. Something was inside the cave. John fell backward in panic, slamming his butt against the tracks. He winced but couldn't tend to the pain. Not now. He limped back to the handcar as fast as he could and released the brake.

"Finally leaving, eh? 'Bout time." Jimmy looked at John. His typical tan was a sickly white. "Dude, what'd you see? What'd you see in there?"

"Pedal," John stammered. "Dude—pedal!"

They raced across the bridge and gained speed as they began to descend. Halfway down the mountain, John's breathing finally settled. John lifted his feet from the pedals. Jimmy did the same, getting a break while the railcar coasted.

Normally, Jimmy acted like a lunatic when the railcar was cruising this fast. He'd wave his arms in the air and shout like it was Independence Day. This time, he didn't even notice the speed. "What'd you see, dude?"

"I don't know, man," John said. "It was just a big shadow, like not a small animal."

Jimmy shook his head and giggled. "I told you we shouldn't have gone up there. In other news, we better pick up the pace. We're running late."

When they reached The Roost, they darted to the Daggon house and jumped in The Fury. Minutes later they slid into the drive-in parking lot on two wheels.

"I love the car," Rachel said as John and Jimmy slammed the doors shut.

"Thanks." John's face reddened. He dropped into a seat beside Shane and across from Rachel and Billy.

"What?" Rachel held her hands up. "I mean it, it's a nice car."

John gave Billy a side eye and tried to hold in his laugh.

"Where's your girl at?" Jimmy asked Shane, as he took a seat at the end of the table.

"She bailed," Shane admitted. "I've been third-wheeling all day."

"Speaking of wheeling, y'all took too long to get here. I can't stay." Billy pointed a thumb toward Rachel. "She's gotta be home by seven, and I got to drop her off."

Rachel stood up and pushed her chair to the table. Billy did the same.

Shane tilted his head. "But she drove here."

"Yeah, well..." Billy stammered and looked at Rachel for help.

"I need him to ride with me," she said. "My dad doesn't like me out by myself at night."

"Who's going to take me home?" Shane asked.

"You live next door to us," Billy said. "Bum a ride from John. Got to go. See y'all at school!"

Billy escorted Rachel to her car. He opened her door for her, closed it gently behind her, then ran around to the passenger side and jumped in.

"They're definitely going to suck face." Shane kissed his hand dramatically for emphasis.

In the midst of Shane's imaginary make-out session, a tan, blue-eyed carhop skated to their table.

"What can I get for you?" she asked.

"Oh—um, hey, Cassie." John fidgeted with the menu nervously. "Uh, I'll do a pretzel."

"Anything else?" she asked, not breaking eye contact.

"Uh, just cheese, I guess. You know, for the, um, pretzel."

"Well, lucky for you, it comes with cheese." Cassie winked and then skated away.

"Dude," John said when he regained his ability to talk, "y'all didn't tell me she worked here!"

Shane and Jimmy looked past John, gaping as Cassie skated back to the kitchen.

"Hello?" John waved his hands in front of Shane and Jimmy, who continued to watch Cassie skate away. "Oh well. Maybe I'll have a class with her at school."

Shane reminded him that Cassie was a grade older. He'd have to take honors classes to have a shot at sharing a classroom with her. And she was smart, probably so smart she'd be in honors classes also, with juniors—not sophomores like John.

John tapped the tabletop and wracked his brain. There had to be a way to get in a class with Cassie. "What if—"

"Here's your pretzel." Cassie faced John with flirty eyes and handed him a paper plate with a giant, cheese-drizzled pretzel on top. "With cheese."

John scrambled for something to say, anything to keep Cassie by his side for another glorious moment. "Thanks, I'm John—John Daggon."

"Cassie Mentz." She hugged her serving tray to her chest.

"Well, it's nice to meet you. I'll see ya around?"

"Yeah." Cassie pushed away from the table and skated off.

Jimmy elbowed John. "Dude, what the heck? I wanted food, man. I'm starving."

"Dude, I panicked! She's hot, and I got nervous. My bad." John bit into his pretzel. Salty and doughy, but not a real dinner. "I need something else anyway. McDonald's?"

That night, John fell asleep replaying his conversation with Cassie over and over in his head.

***

In the morning, John and Billy raced out the door as the sun began to peek over the horizon, casting Burdine in a soft glow. Billy floored The Fury, leaving the driveway in a cloud of gravel dust.

"So," John said while rolling down his window, "you and Rachel have fun last night?"

Billy turned on the radio. "I'm going to ask her out officially this weekend."

"I knew it!" John slapped his hand on the dashboard.

"Don't say a word to anybody." Billy tweaked the radio tuner until he found a station with good reception. "I mean anybody, not even Jimmy or Shane."

They pulled into the school parking lot before the song had a chance to finish. Billy killed the engine, and Jimmy and Shane walked toward them. Billy grabbed John's shirtsleeve. "Not a word."

"So, you have fun last night, Billy?" Shane teased.

"Shut up, dude. We're going to be late." Billy tossed his backpack over his shoulder. "Come on."

The four walked past the big bear statue to the front

doors, each glancing up at the old clock on the wall. They made it before the first bell.

"Ahhhh!" Shane inhaled deeply. "New year, same crap smell."

The group busted out laughing before going their separate ways. John headed to Honors Mathematics with Mrs. Skipper, where he settled into a desk in the back left corner. He scanned the room and met his first disappointment. No Cassie.

The hour dragged by as John stared at the board in confusion. He felt totally lost. Even worse, he was bummed Cassie wasn't in his class.

Two more class periods passed.

Jimmy, Shane, and Billy gathered at a lunch table, waiting on John.

"Dude, where is he?" Jimmy glanced at his watch. "Lunch started like ten minutes ago."

Billy pointed toward the front of the lunchroom, where John walked in. Billy, Shane, and Jimmy tracked John as he made his plate, then took his spot at the table.

"Oh, man, Mrs. Goodman would not shut up." John opened a ketchup packet and squirted it on a small mound of tater tots. "She talked for like five minutes after the bell rung."

"What are you doing in her class?" Shane snatched a tater tot from John's tray. "Oh, wait! Don't tell me you signed up for honors English."

Jimmy shook his head. "You're an idiot, dude!"

Billy took a sip of water. "I don't get it. What's so funny?"

"Your brother the genius signed up for all honors

classes," Shane said. "He hoped he'd wind up in a class with Cassie Mentz."

"Well," Billy said, "any luck?"

"Nope." John shoveled a forkful of corn into his mouth.

The other three slapped the table and cackled and punched John lightly. John just kept eating.

By the last class of the day, John had lost all hope of sharing a classroom with his crush.

A black-haired, bespectacled man stood in front of the classroom and introduced himself as Mr. Buckles. "I see you all saved the best class for last," he said. "Welcome to Honors History."

John half-listened while he surveyed the room before letting out a sigh. Still no Cassie.

Mr. Buckles didn't seem to notice John's heartache. He just went on like it was another normal day. "Let's not waste any time," he continued. "Turn your books to—"

The classroom door opened. Mr. Buckles stopped in mid-sentence. A tan, curly-headed beauty stepped in. It was Cassie!

She whispered an apology to Mr. Buckles and walked to the back of the room, claiming the lone empty desk beside John. John wiggled out of his slouched posture and sat up straight.

"As I was saying," Mr. Buckles continued, "turn your books to page eight."

John looked at the textbook the remainder of class, but his brain was elsewhere. He spent the whole hour trying to come up with something clever to say to Cassie, but his brain failed him, and the bell rang. He stuffed his book into his backpack and faced Cassie.

"Well," he said, "time for basketball practice." It was the best he could do. Not clever or memorable, but it would have to work.

Cassie took the bait. "I didn't know you played."

"Yep, well I haven't played here yet. We..." His brain threatened to shortcut. "We, uh, we just moved here like a month ago."

"You're new to town." Cassie raised her eyebrows. "That's why I never saw you before the day on the lake."

John told himself to breathe. "Oh," he said nonchalantly, "you were there when I jumped?"

"Yes," she patted his shoulder, "you literally looked at me before you jumped!"

"Oh yeah, well...I hit so hard I don't remember much from that day, but I do remember you from the drive-in." The words sprinted out of his mouth in a single breath. "Solid pretzel by the way."

Cassie shrugged. "It's the cheese, that's what makes it."

John suggested she come to a game. "I mean, we don't have one for like another month, but you should definitely come watch."

Cassie said she probably should and made her way to the front of the classroom. John trailed close behind.

"Hey," he said, "we should be partners. You know, if like we have to do a project or something."

"Okay." She walks backward and keeps her eyes on John. "Sure, we can do that."

John waves goodbye and heads to the gym, berating himself for lack of suavity. Once he changed into his practice uniform, he met Billy on the baseline and told him about Cassie. Billy patted him on the back as Coach Jenkins walked across the gym floor.

"Guys, we've added two more players to our roster, Billy and John Daggon. I expect you all to welcome the Daggon brothers and build chemistry with them on and off the floor. After all, we're one team with the same goal: We want to win." Coach crossed his arms over his belly and rocked back and forth. "That said, the past few years are behind us. We're done being a losing program. We're done being the laughing stock of the Frisco Conference. Our first game is a month away, so let's get to work!"

***

Basketball season started with four straight road games. Somehow, the Bruins won them all. Everyone was shocked, claiming it was the best start since the early thirties. John and Billy weren't sure if that was accurate, but they didn't care. It felt good to be part of something positive.

The first home game was coming up, and everyone at school planned to be there.

*Well,* John wrote in his journal, *everyone but Cassie.* She had to work, but she asked John to come by afterward and tell her all about it. The pair talked almost every day, but mostly just about school stuff. They partnered up on a history project, and John was still unsure whether Cassie was interested in him beyond his academic abilities.

With a win against Rolla High, it would be the best start in school history. There was just one problem. Rolla were the defending state champs and had won two of the last three against Burdine.

The night of the game, Mr. Daggon was stuck at work. It happened a lot, but he insisted it wouldn't be that way forever. He flipped on the radio in his office.

*Goooooood evening, ladies and gentlemen. This is Carl Ables from 97.1 The Bruin, and I am here with my cohost, Cecil Edwards. We are broadcasting live from The Den, the home gym of the Burdine Bruins! Tonight, the Bruins look to start the season five-and-oh for the first time ever, but it will be a difficult task as they host the reigning state champs, the Rolla Bulldogs.*

Mr. Daggon filed a document and turned the volume up on the radio.

*But what a great start to the year this has been already for the Bruins. After a rough season last year, the expectations were not very high.*

*I don't think anyone was expecting this kind of start, Carl. However, here we are, undefeated. I will say, this will definitely be the toughest opponent the Bruins have faced so far. Let me ask you, Carl, what has changed for the Bruins that has allowed them to find some success this year?*

*Well, stating the obvious, it's the Daggon brothers. This time last year, this town had no clue who these boys were—that includes you, Cecil. But now I am sure everyone knows their names.*

*The older brother, Billy Daggon, comes into*

Mr. Daggon pushed back in his desk chair. He knew his boys were good. Hearing the radio commentators confirmed it.

Inside the gym, the crowd poured in. As the team warmed up, John gazed up in the bleachers at the rowdy crowd.

Billy thumped his little brother on the chest. "Come on, Johnny, lock in."

John took a last look at the crowd, where Jimmy and Shane cheered and waved. John gave them a head nod, then regathered his focus on the game.



     Brock Enloe

*at four-and-oh. There's the jump ball, and we are underway! Rolla wins the tip and immediately dribbles down and buries a three. Burdine inbounds it, and John Daggon brings the ball up for the Bruins. He swings the ball to Billy Daggon, who pump fakes, drives in, and lays it up. The basket counts and the foul.*

Mr. Daggon pumped a fist in the air and leaned forward in his chair.

"Sir, the last train has made it into the station."

Mr. Daggon looked up to see one of his assistants standing expectantly at his door. "Come on in," he said, "let's update the train log." He reached to the end of his desk and turned the radio off.

Soon as the meeting ended and the assistant exited, Mr. Daggon cut the radio back on. Carl and Cecil were practically shouting to be heard over the crowd.

*Alright folks, we are all tied up here with fifteen seconds to go in the fourth quarter. What a game it has been.*

*Carl, the Daggon brothers have been something else tonight. Billy has thirty-one points, and John seventeen. I would expect the Bruins to get Billy the last shot here and see if he can seal off his stellar night with a game-winner.*

*And here we go. John brings the ball up for the Bruins. Fifteen, fourteen, thirteen... He passes it to the wing, who immediately swings it to Billy Daggon. Billy dribbles back up top and motions for everyone to clear out. Ten, nine, eight... Billy drives*

*right, spins left, and goes up for the shot. Drawing
two defenders, he sees his brother, John, cut to the
backside block. Billy passes it. John catches and goes
up. It's in! Burdine goes up two with three seconds.
Rolla doesn't have any time-outs left, so they inbound
quickly. The guard takes two quick dribbles and
heaves up a nearly full-court shot, and…it's no good!
Burdine wins, Burdine wins!*

*What a night for the Daggon brothers, Carl!*
*What a night for Burdine!*

Mr. Daggon listened with pride as the announcers recapped the game's most important stats. Billy led the Bruins with thirty-one points, while John had nineteen, including the game-winning lay-up. The Bruins moved to five-and-oh for the first time in school history, courtesy of two new kids from North Carolina.

At the school, fans flooded the gym floor and rushed the team in celebration. It was madness for a few minutes, and then the crowd calmed down as the team headed to the locker room.

A few minutes later, John and Billy walked out, arm in arm. Jimmy and Shane congratulated them and solemnly swore to never miss a game as long as the Daggon boys were around. The group pushed the double doors open as a voice called out behind them.

"You guys played so great!" Rachel wrapped her arms around Billy's neck. "Y'all want to go celebrate?"

Jimmy and Shane declined. It was already dark outside, and Shane was in trouble for failing a test the week before. He had to beg his parents to even go to the game.

                    Brock Enloe

Rachel considered John.

"Um," he mumbled, "you two go ahead. I got something I got to do as well."

Billy squeezed Rachel. "Looks like it's just you and me, babe." He tossed a set of keys to John. "She'll drop me off at home, so you get The Fury for the night. Take good care of her."

John shoved the keys in his pocket and checked his watch. *Forty-five minutes 'til closing*, he thought. He got to the drive-in diner in near-record time and messed his sweaty hair in the rearview mirror before hopping out.

Cassie already had a pretzel ready. She brought it to his table and sat down. "Soooo, how'd it go?"

"Well, we won." John held up his pretzel. "I had nineteen points, including the game winner."

Cassie's jaw dropped. "Oh my! Congratulations! I hate I missed it, but I—"

"You had to work. I get it, and it's okay! You can just catch the next game."

Cassie promised she'd do everything in her power to get off work for the next game. "It's been soooo slow tonight," she groaned. "We should've just closed."

"Fortunately," John said, "you've only got thirty minutes or so 'til close, right?"

"Yeah, but I have to wait until my mom gets off. We share a car and she works late," Cassie said with a pout, "so I'll be here a while."

"No, you won't." It was the opening John had been looking for. He wanted to jump for joy but knew he had to play it cool. "There's no need for you to sit here all alone. I can take you home."

Cassie perked up. "Are you sure?"

"Of course! As long as you can tolerate smelling me the whole ride home. I'm still sweaty from the game."

"Okay, stinky, I'll call my mom's work and let her know." Cassie ran across the parking lot to the kitchen door. She pulled it open and called over her shoulder, "Thank you so much!"

John wanted to thank her for the opportunity. Instead, he sat still and practiced keeping his leg from shaking with excitement. Thirty minutes later, the diner's exterior lights flickered off, and Cassie strolled toward John. He held out one hand and introduced The Fury.

"The Fury?" she laughed.

John started The Fury, backed out of his parking place, and turned up the radio.

"You don't strike me as an Outfield guy."

"What?" John felt Cassie's eyes on him. They burned, but in a good way. "I freaking love The Outfield! And this song is awesome!"

Tony Lewis poured out his heart on the radio, belting out "Alone With You," saying everything John was too nervous to say.

"I prefer The Police," Cassie said, "but The Outfield is pretty rad too, I guess." She turned to look out the passenger window, watching the night pass by.

The music played as small talk turned into deeper, more meaningful conversation. The fifteen-minute drive felt like thirty seconds as The Fury's headlights cut through a patch of trees and lit up a two-story brick house.

"Well, this is me. Thank you again for the ride." Cassie's voice was soft and uncertain. She curled a strand

          Brock Enloe

of hair around a finger.

"Yeah, no problem."

John looked at Cassie, and everything froze. Time stood still. Their eyes locked. An acorn dropped onto the windshield and broke the spell.

"Um, let me walk you to the door." John leapt out of the car to open Cassie's door.

"Thanks for saving me from boredom tonight," Cassie said. "I had fun with you."

"Yeah, me too." John put his thumbs in his pockets. "And the pretzel was good, as always."

The two stood on Cassie's front porch and gazed into each other's eyes. Then John moved toward the girl deemed out of his league. He pulled her close, brushed a strand of hair out of Cassie's face, and leaned in for a kiss. She followed his lead, moving her pursed lips toward his.

A terrifying screech echoed out of the darkness. John and Cassie opened their eyes in fear.

"What was that?" Cassie asked, her voice nearly inaudible.

John shook his head. Was the sound connected to Shane's mountain bat stories? "You should probably get in for the night," John said. "You know, just to be safe."

Cassie jammed the key into the lock, turned the handle, and pushed the door open.

"I'll see you tomorrow," John said.

"Yeah, see you tomorrow. Be safe!"

Still spooked by the noise, John sprinted back to The Fury and sped off into the night, wondering if they would get a chance to complete their near kiss in the future.

# CHAPTER 3

# THE ATTACK

"Listen up, boys." Coach Jenkins paced in front of his team after practice. "Last week we beat Rolla and improved to five-and-oh. But last week is behind us. This week starts the Annual Frisco Fall Classic, sixteen teams competing to raise up one trophy. This tournament has no effect on playoffs or conference rankings, but Burdine has never won this tournament. I think this is our year to change that. We've already set one school record, let's set another one. We had a great practice today. Now go home, rest up, and be ready to go. First round is tomorrow. Win that game and we host Friday's game for a spot in the final four. Break it down, and y'all get out of here."

The team piled their hands on top of one another.

"1,2,3 Bruins!"

John and Billy changed out of their practice uniforms and rushed to meet Jimmy and Shane at The Roost.

"Aye, there they are!" Shane shouted in Pirate.

"What's up, boys!" Billy called out.

Jimmy threw a peace sign.

"Just chatting about the incident," Shane said.

"The incident?" John asked.

"Happened last Thursday night near Riverbend Drive," Shane said. "They found some person's body all bloodied and mangled."

John winced and asked if it was true. Jimmy insisted it was true, and it happened after the game the week before.

"The news won't say it," Shane said, "but had to be a mountain bat."

"Dude, shut up man!" Jimmy grabbed a pebble off the ground and chucked it at Shane. "It ain't a joke. My dad said the person probably was drunk and stumbled on the tracks."

"Wait." John's voice shook. "You said Riverbend Drive?"

"Yeah," Shane responded. "Why?"

John lowered himself to the edge of the couch. "As crazy as it sounds, Shane may be right. I took Cassie home that night, and—"

"You're telling me you were at Cassie Mentz's house?" Shane pushed John off the couch. "I don't need to hear the rest of your story. I don't believe it, not one bit."

Jimmy and Billy grinned at Shane.

"Believe what you want, but I was there—promise!" John brushed off the back of his shorts. "We were standing on her porch, and we heard this loud screech belt out from the darkness."

The boys looked at each other, trying to figure out if

they should buy Shane's stories about the mountain bat or John's story about being on Cassie's porch.

"I'm telling the truth!" John kicked at the floor. "I went to the drive-in diner after the game and ended up taking Cassie home from work because her mom had to work late. I walked her to the front door and we were about to kiss. That's when we heard it!"

Jimmy doubled over in laughter. Billy dropped his head into his hands. Shane looked at John with a glint in his eye.

"Alright, dude, now I know it's fake." Shane laughed. "You being on Cassie Mentz's porch was hard enough to believe, but you and her about to kiss? Yeah, I'm calling B.S."

"Let's pretend your story was true, bro—well, maybe not the kissing part," Jimmy joked. "The noise you heard was probably just the train slamming on the brakes before hitting that guy."

Billy shrugged. "That's the only logical explanation."

***

In the final class of the day, John ignored Mr. Buckles' lecture on the late 1920s. He was too busy passing notes to Cassie.

*You coming to the game tonight?*

Cassie smirked, wrote a little something, and passed the note back.

*Can't, have work! But I promise I'll come to the next one :)*

Right before class ended, John passed her a final note.



Before Cassie opened the note, the intercom sounded: *Will the boys' basketball team please make their way to the bus out front at this time? Good luck, guys, in the first round of the Frisco Classic.*

John threw his books in his bag and stood up. Cassie handed the note back and mouthed, "Good luck."

Making his way to the front of the school, John opened the note and held his breath.



***

In the Annual Frisco Fall Fest Classic, Burdine High beat Thayer Tuesday in the first round, then upset Sale Creek at home. Cassie got Friday night off and came to the next game, but John only scored twelve. The Bruins were up big by halftime, so Coach pulled the starters to keep them fresh for the semi-final game against the Painter Panthers.

After the last victory, the upperclassmen threw a bonfire party on the mountain. John felt conflicted and wrote about the whole thing in his journal.

Everyone invited got the same firm instructions: Park on the back side of the park, away from the ranger's hut.



Billy and Rachel rode to the party with Shane and Jimmy. Cassie had to work since she took off the night before, so John offered to pick her up when her shift ended, even if it meant he'd be late to the party. She took him up on the offer.



John leaned back in his chair to check the clock. It was already seven forty-five. "Oh shoot!" He barely avoided tipping over backward in his chair. He tossed his journal under his bed, pulled on his favorite pair of faded blue jeans, a white t-shirt, and his navy Members Only jacket.

He sped the whole trip, fixed his blonde curls on the way, and only arrived five minutes late.

Cassie stood up from her seat. She pushed her bottom lip out pitifully. "I thought you forgot about me."

"How could I forget about you?" John asked as Cassie got in The Fury.

"So," Cassie asked, "is this the date you referred to in your note?"

"Definitely not. I just couldn't wait to see you."

From Cassie's response, the phrase came out as cool as it sounded in John's head. He pushed the pedal to the floorboard until they reached the party. Embers leapt from the fire and burned high in the sky, glowing red one

                    Brock Enloe

last time before blending into the gray smoke dancing above the trees.

John took Cassie by the hand and helped her out of the car. As they approached the bonfire, Shane and Jimmy waved them over.

"It's about time you got here!" Jimmy said.

John nodded.

"Oh, so you weren't lying the other night at The Roost." Shane pointed at John's hand, which was wrapped around Cassie's.

John scoffed and squeezed Cassie's hand.

"Cassie," Shane blurted out, "I just want you to know that John has been talking about you non-stop since the day on the lake when he first saw you."

"Dude!" John hit Shane on the shoulder, which sent Shane and Jimmy into riotous laughter.

Cassie took a step away from John, though she kept hold of his hand. "I thought you didn't remember me from that day?"

"What's up, little brother?" Billy sidled up beside John and put a hand on his shoulder.

John greeted Billy with a bro hug and thanked him for letting him use The Fury.

Billy looked at John's outstretched arm, which still had Cassie attached. "So, this is the girl my brother has been talking about."

John looked down, his face glowing red.

"Hey, I'm Cassie." Cassie blushed and curtsied to Billy and Rachel.

"And where have y'all been?" Shane eyed Billy with suspicion.

"Oh, you know," Billy said with a smirk, "the woods."

They sat down and gazed at the stars, while the fire crackled and popped. It was the first time they'd all been together as a group, but they already seemed like family.

The brothers shared stories from their time in North Carolina, Jimmy and Shane reminisced about growing up in Burdine, and the girls laughed off wrong opinions they had toward one another all these years.

As the fire died down, Tommy stood up. He was an upperclassman, one of the guys who lost playing time to the Daggon brothers. But he didn't seem to mind. He liked winning.

"Listen up!" he shouted. "I just wanted to thank everyone for coming out tonight. I think the whole team would agree with me when I say that we appreciate your support. This year is off to a great start, but we aren't done yet. Next week we beat Painter and move on to the Fall Fest Classic championship! Now, let's party!"

The other seniors dumped gasoline on the fire, making it burn painfully bright and dangerously high. Tommy spun the volume knob on the radio, cranking it to full blast.

John and Billy raised their cups in the air, as everyone got up to dance. Cassie got to her feet to join them but began to cough. John led her away, toward the woods, for some fresh air.

Just past the tree line, John asked Cassie if she was okay. She raised both thumbs.

They kept walking. The music faded in the background, and John looked up. "It's magical, almost."

"What is?"

        Brock Enloe

"The stars." He pointed at the sky. "Where we lived in North Carolina, you couldn't see many. The lights along the coast interfered. But here, it's like you can see the whole galaxy."

Cassie grabbed his hand. "I'm glad you moved here."

Hand in hand, they talked and walked deep into the woods, until they came to an overlook. Below was the well-lit town of Burdine. A subtle breeze crept through the trees and spilled over the cliff. It was the only sound for a long time.

Then, John nervously murmured, "I like you."

Cassie admitted she liked John as well. Then, John gently lifted Cassie's chin, leaned in, and finished the kiss he started on her porch a week earlier. As their lips separated, something rustled in the bushes.

"Oh, my goodness," Cassie huffed, "we hear something every time!"

John licked his lips. "Yeah, well at least it was after we kissed this time." He squinted toward the bushes. "We probably should get back to the party."

The two retraced their steps, relishing the lingering effects of the kiss. Then they heard the noise again, only this time it came from the trees above.

John looked up in the trees and turned in circles, trying to spot whatever hid in the shadows above. Something was wrong. He felt it in his gut. They needed to get out of the woods. Cassie felt it too.

"I can see the fire." Her voice quaked. "Let's, let's just get back to the party."

John took her hand, as a loud screech cried out from the night sky, ringing through the forest—the same screech they heard on Cassie's porch.

"Run!" John tugged at Cassie's hand.

But it was too late. A giant winged creature swooped down out of the darkness and dug its talons into John, driving him to the ground. Cassie tumbled and watched helplessly as the creature slashed John's chest with its long, clawlike fingers. Blood splashed the ground.

"RUN!" John repeated. He spewed blood from his mouth and tried to wrestle the creature off him.

Cassie sprinted toward the party. "Help! Someone, please—help! HELP!"

Tommy killed the radio and looked toward the woods, one hand over his eyes. Cassie rushed out of the woods at him.

"It's attacking John," she cried. "Please help!"

Tommy stood dumbfounded, processing what Cassie said. Billy didn't process anything. He took off into the woods with Jimmy and Shane close behind.

Through the dark, they spotted the giant, winged predator on top of John. The grotesque creature bent over and buried its fangs in John's neck. Billy reached down and grabbed a handful of stones, then hurled them at the beast, cursing it loudly.

Shane and Jimmy joined in, pelting the attacker repeatedly. One of the rocks ricocheted off the creature's head. It let go of John and faced the boys, hissing and flashing its fangs that were drenched in John's blood.

"Oh shoot, it's pissed!" Shane reached down for another rock. As he reared back to launch it at the beast, light flooded through the woods.

Jimmy turned to see the park ranger leap out of his

truck and aim a gun into the sky. "Hit the ground!" Jimmy shouted.

The ranger pulled the trigger, sending a flare into the night sky. The creature recoiled at the bright flash and loud noise, then backed into the darkness and disappeared.

Billy rushed to John's side and fell to the ground beside him. "John, John, you okay? Stay with me, dude!"

Cassie and Rachel stood nearby, hugging each other, as Billy and Shane lifted John and carried him to the ranger's truck. Shane took off his shirt and held it against John's neck to stop the bleeding.

When they reached the truck, all six friends piled in. Cassie and Rachel squeezed in the passenger front seat, and the others crammed in the back seat, with John laid over their laps.

The ranger hesitated before getting in. "Everyone, go home!" he yelled at the remaining partygoers. "You know you're not supposed to be here after dark!"

Then he banged the truck into gear and rushed down the mountain, throwing red and blue lights on the fir trees along the way. In the backseat, John faded in and out of consciousness. Billy held John's head and reassured him all would be well.

"Ranger, what was that thing?" Shane demanded.

The ranger tightened his lips and focused on the road ahead.

"Why won't you tell us what that was?" Shane begged.

*** 

The next morning, everyone was talking about the

attack. Janet Killingsworth, anchor with Burdine News Channel 9 found the ranger on duty and interviewed him. According to Ranger Harris, John was attacked by a bat.

"The teens knew better than to be up on the mountain after dark, and we will be stricter on the state park closings from here on out," Ranger Harris said. "With that being said, our thoughts and prayers are with John and his family."

# CHAPTER 4

# THE FRISCO FINAL FOUR

After spending the night in the hospital, John was discharged. The doctors couldn't find a reason to keep him around. They'd rushed him into the operating room for emergency surgery, but by the time they had him under anesthesia, there was nothing left to do. It baffled the surgeon. He'd seen a series of deep lacerations on John's face and a couple gashes in his throat before he scrubbed in for surgery. Then, nothing. Another doctor gave John a couple shots and a quick blood transfusion and sent him on his way.

A couple days later, John sat in his room, documenting the whole thing in his journal, doing his best to remember what happened so he could process it all.

> The doc swore my neck was gushing blood, and when he went to fix it, it had already miraculously healed itself. Said he'd never seen anything like it in all his years. Doesn't make sense to me, but

I'm glad to be home.

Speaking of home, Mom pretty much has me on house arrest. She brings me meal after meal and tells me to lie down and take it easy. The first few days were kind of nice, but now I'm starting to go stir crazy.

Truthfully, I feel fine. My neck still stings, but the cuts and scrapes have healed for the most part. And I know it sounds crazy, but I feel stronger, faster. And I think it's more than a feeling. When I looked in the mirror this morning, my muscles were more toned than ever. But who knows? Maybe the attack messed with my vision.

It definitely messed with John's athletic eligibility. Despite John's rapid recovery, the doctor wouldn't clear John to play in the semifinals. John understood. It hadn't even been a week since the attack. But he felt great, so he was going to do his best to get permission to play in the championship if the Bruins made it that far.

His next doctor's appointment was set for the following day. Until then, he had more pressing concerns.

The nightmares have been terrible. Every time I close my eyes, I see that thing. I can still see the deep yellow eyes, the long pointy ears, the flared nose, and the sharp fangs painted red with blood. The terrifying screech echoes in my head as I picture the black finger-like talons ripping through my skin.

The last thing I see before waking up is the

          Brock Enloe

thing spreading its leathery wings to take flight, leaving me lying bloody on the ground below.

The news said it was a bat, but I've seen bats in North Carolina, and they're like scrawny rats with wings. This thing was bigger than me, and I'm 5'11". Everyone who saw it agrees it wasn't a bat, but no one knows exactly what it was. Shane insists that it was a mountain bat, but he can't even explain what a mountain bat is.

When it was real close to me, I noticed it had a face that looked almost

John nibbled on the end of his pen before he quickly finished his sentence:

human.

He ended the entry reminiscing about kissing Cassie, then closed his journal. The doorbell rang.

"Cassie is here!" Mrs. Daggon yelled.

Hearing her name made John's heart race. He rushed out of his room to greet her. "Hey!" he said. "What are you doing here?"

"I asked her to sit with you while your dad and I go to the game," Mrs. Daggon explained.

"Really?"

"Yep!" Cassie grinned.

"We should be home before eight," Mrs. Daggon said. "I left some cash on the counter, so you guys can order Pizza Inn and rent a movie. Have fun."

Mr. Daggon grabbed the car keys and eyed John and Cassie. "And behave."

As soon as the station wagon was out of view, John went to his room to change clothes. He was in his pajamas, not exactly the best clothing for a hot, stay-at-home date.

"So," Cassie said from outside John's closed bedroom door, "what movie do you want to rent?"

John slipped on a pair of jeans and stepped into a pair of sneakers. "I'm movied out," he said. "That's all I've done these past few days. *Bloodsport*, *Jaws 2*, *Predator*, I've literally watched them all. I have a better idea." He slung his pajama shirt at the laundry basket, reached into the closet for a clean shirt, and pulled open his bedroom door.

"Okay, let me hear it," she said, taking in John's shirtless physique.

"I got a special place I want to show you."

"Uhhh, no. Your mom specifically said to not let you leave the house."

John pulled the clean Polo shirt over his head and poked his hands through the arm holes. "It's right behind the house. Cassie, please! I've been cooped up in this house for days. I'm going crazy."

Cassie watched John smooth the front of his shirt with one hand. "Fine," she agreed, "but we're not going off this property, so don't get any funny ideas in your head."

John grabbed her hand. "You're the best!"

After a few minutes of ducking and dodging, weaving and walking, they stood in the clearing in the middle of the woods. The abandoned depot stood before them.

"Come on!" John opened the front door of the old depot. "Welcome to The Roost!"

"What is this place?" Cassie scanned inside the old building.

"An old train depot cabin that is now our hangout spot, a.k.a. The Roost."

"The Roost?" Cassie asked.

John started to explain the origin of the name, but Cassie cut him off. "That's okay," she said. "It's really cool here, but we need to get back to the house now."

"Wait!" John waltzed across The Roost and pulled the cover off the handcar. It sat on a small piece of track that went from the middle of The Roost to the long stretch of abandoned railroad track outside. "You've got to take a ride first."

Cassie crossed her arms. "John, we can't. Your mom told me we were not to leave the house. You just got out of the hospital. Look, I want to go for a ride on that cart thing, but..."

"But what?" John rubbed the handcar handles.

"I really like you." Cassie bit her lip. "And I want your mom to like me, too."

John put a hand on Cassie's cheek. "I really like you, too," he said, "and I promise I'm okay. Besides, we'll be back before they get home."

Cassie put up a brief fight, but it ended in a kiss. Then John muscled the handcar out of The Roost along the abandoned railroad, helped Cassie onto it, and began to pedal.

The first ten minutes on the tracks featured John explaining the upgrades he and Jimmy made to the railcar. On the outskirts of town, Cassie finally had a chance to say something.

"This is literally so awesome!"

"Just wait," John said, "you ain't seen nothing yet."

The town shrunk behind them, as the tracks led back into dense forest alongside the river. Cassie's eyes traced the tracks that curved through the trees and paused on the iron bridge standing tall between the mountains.

"That's where we are going?" she asked.

"Bingo." John reached behind his seat with a grunt and started up the railcar's little engine. "Just sit back and enjoy the ride. We'll be there in no time."

Cassie sighed. The sound of water trickling over rocks climbed up the mountainside. The clicking handcar climbed its way up in elevation. Wind blew through the trees that were slowly falling away underneath the tracks.

"Oh, I almost forgot." John pushed the power button on the stereo. "Earth Angel" began to play.

"Smooth," Cassie joked. She took John's hand and relaxed as they neared the peak.

John killed the engine and pedaled to the middle of the iron bridge. He pulled the hand brake hard to make sure the handcar wouldn't move, then stood up. "Here we are," he said. "Best view in all of Burdine."

Cassie didn't reply. She just gazed out over the trees and town below.

"Better than staying home watching movies, right?" John eased himself back to his seat on the handcar.

"Definitely."

Their lips met and smooshed together through three more songs and a commercial break.

*And we're live here for the semi-final game between the Painter Panthers and the Burdine Bruins.*

　　　　　　Brock Enloe

*Winner advances to the championship game, which will be held Saturday night.*

John's eyes popped open. He grinned as Cassie wiped her lips with a shirtsleeve. "I brought you up here for the view," he said, "but the past fifteen minutes you had your eyes closed."

Cassie rolled her eyes. John turned up the radio.

*The Bruins will be without starting point guard, John Daggon, today. They will need a big game from his older brother and lead scorer, Billy Daggon, if they expect to play on Saturday.*

John and Cassie dangled their feet from the iron bridge. Behind them, the Bruins scratched and clawed away for nearly thirty-two minutes. Ahead of them, the sun reflected off the lake.

*We're all tied up at eighty-seven with six seconds to go. It all comes down to this play, Burdine with the ball. A quick inbound to Billy Daggon, who pushes it up the court. Five, four, three— He stops to pull from way outside the arc. It's up, and it's good! Billy Daggon with the dagger in the Panthers' heart! Bruins win it, ninety to eighty-seven!*

"Let's go!!!" John jumped to his feet and threw his fists into the air. His voice bounced off the canyon below.

*Billy Daggon finishes with fifty-one points and books the Bruins a spot in the championship game this Saturday night. Thank you, guys, for listening. We will see you all this Saturday!*

*A Bat Among Bruins*

John's celebration continued until he fell to the ground. He held his head and moaned.

"John, what's wrong?"

John breathed heavy, slow breaths, as the pain eased.

"That's it," Cassie said, helping John to his feet. "We are going home. Your mom is going to kill me!"

John assured Cassie that he was okay and started the handcar back down the mountain. The stress of the situation melted away when he placed a hand on Cassie's leg. They hurried from The Roost to John's house, then plopped down on the couch and cut on the TV just before John's parents burst through the front door.

"What a game!" Mr. Daggon said. "We won!"

Mrs. Daggon clapped excitedly and went into the kitchen. John high-fived his dad and explained that he and Cassie caught the game on the radio.

"You guys didn't use the cash on the counter?" Mrs. Daggon held out the bills left on the counter. "What did you all eat?"

John admitted they didn't eat.

"John Daggon, you better feed this poor girl," his mother said. "I am sure she is hungry."

John took the cash, then rushed to the station wagon with Cassie by his side.

"You think your mom knows?" Cassie asked.

"Nah," John replied. "Now, where do you want to eat? I still owe you that date, remember?"

The indecisive couple drove around aimlessly until eventually settling on a restaurant on Main Street. Compared to the taste of Cassie's lips, the food was flavorless. But he forced down a hamburger and fries before driving Cassie home.

With night descending, John reached into the backseat of his parents' family car. "Let's take a picture." He held up his mom's Polaroid camera.

Cassie scooted across the bench seat. John wrapped his right arm around her shoulder and pulled her close.

"Say cheese!"

The camera flashed and spit out the black-and-white rectangle. John snatched it with his right hand and started shaking it in the air. He turned his body to keep the photo out of Cassie's view.

"Let me see!" Cassie cried, pulling at John's shoulder to get a view of the photo.

John laughed and promised to show the photo when it was ready. He counted out loud to ten, then inspected the photo.

Something was wrong. John shook the photo faster. He looked at the photo again, and a cold chill ran down his spine.

"John, you look sick," Cassie said. "What's wrong?"

"I, uh..." John folded the photo and shoved it deep into his pants pocket. "I look terrible. It's a terrible picture, embarrassing."

Cassie raised an eyebrow. "If it's so bad I can't even see it, let's take another."

"Can't, uh, I'm out of film." John tossed the camera into the backseat and leaned in to kiss Cassie.

"Are you the master of distraction or what?" Cassie pushed John away playfully.

"We'll take another picture on our next date, deal?" John said.

Cassie agreed, then kissed John before getting out of the car. He watched as she walked away and into her house.

His mind raced faster than the station wagon and sweat lined his forehead. At home, he stumbled out of the car and crept through the front door, past his parents and into his room. He closed his bedroom door softly, dropped to his bed, and pulled out the folded picture from his pocket. Cassie smiled back at him from the photo. He was nowhere to be seen.

Something slammed against the bedroom door, and it swung open.

"Dude, we won!" Billy raised his arms in victory.

John tucked the photo under his leg before responding, "Dude I know!" He shifted his leg to make sure the photo didn't peek out. "Cassie and I listened. You balled out, man—fifty-one points!"

Billy mimed a three-pointer, ruffled John's curly hair, and headed to bathroom for a much-needed shower. John fell back on his bed and exhaled, debating whether or not to tell Billy about the Polaroid problem.

***

The next afternoon, John sat upright on the examination table at the hospital. One of the doctors who cared for John after the attack checked his vitals and examined his face and neck. John was antsy, hungry to get on the basketball court for the championship game. Mrs. Daggon reminded the doctor that the attack happened less than a week earlier, but he shrugged it off.

 Brock Enloe

"He's healed significantly faster than we ever could have anticipated. I believe he's good to go." The doctor draped the stethoscope around his neck and jotted something in John's medical file. "I mean, his body responded better than the average person to all the tests. However, at the end of the day, you are the mother."

Mrs. Daggon shifted on her chair.

"I'm giving him the green light," the doctor continued, "but you can decide whether you let him play or not."

John's eyes pleaded with his mom in the hospital. Then, his mouth did the same on the car ride back to school. Mrs. Daggon didn't reply until they pulled up to the Burdine High parking lot.

"Well," she said finally, "if Coach decides you're good to go, then I guess I'll let you play."

"Oh, Mom—you're the best!" John hugged his mom, slung his bag over his shoulder, and practically skipped all the way to history class.

"Thought you were pulling a no-show today," Cassie joked as John took his seat beside her.

"I wish," he said. "I had the check-up with the doctor. I'm cleared to play tomorrow."

Cassie's jaw dropped. "Already? How could—"

"Okay everyone, we're going to the library to begin our research projects." Mr. Buckles stood up and put both hands on his desk. "Pick a partner, and on your way out, I'll give you your topics."

Cassie and John approached Mr. Buckles. He handed them a paper that read, *D-Day: Invading Normandy.*

In the library, Cassie dropped her bag by the microfiche station and walked to the card catalog to begin the search for books regarding WWII. John scanned the microfiche archives and found a file with newspapers from around the world. He grabbed the June 1944 file, then grabbed a box of microfiche labeled *Burdine Post 1941–1948*.

His heart pounded in his ears. He looked over his shoulders. No one was watching. He slid the first *Burdine Post* microfiche into the machine and quickly scrolled through the pages. Nothing caught his eye. He grabbed another with the same result, then two more.

He nearly jumped out of his seat when someone touched his neck. It was Cassie. She winked and walked toward the bookshelf labeled 900–999. John turned back to the machine and brought a new microfiche into focus. He scrolled through the pages and then stopped at an article titled "Burdine and the History of the Frisco Railroad."

He zoomed in for a closer look.

*Burdine, Missouri, was established in 1877. At this time, however, it was nothing more than a rural town that sat along the border of the Indian reservation. But in the late 1920s, the Frisco Railroad Company swindled over half the territory from the native Americans. They planned to extend the railroad south, passing up and through the mountains.*

*The native Americans pleaded with the town, warning them of the mountain bats that dwelled inside the cliffs. The town leaders, knowing the profit this would bring, backed the expansion.*

*By fall of 1930, the railroad was open.*

          Brock Enloe

There it was, in black and grey: Mountain bats, just like Shane and Jimmy said.

John printed the article, shoved it into his bag, and put the *Burdine Post* box back. Then he tossed on a microfiche from the *New York Times* and printed out the first article he found on the invasion of Normandy. It slowly spit out of the printer as Cassie walked up.

She slammed a stack of books on the table. "Ready to work?"

That night, John wrote in his journal and rubbed his neck. All his other wounds were healed, but the two puncture wounds remained in place. They didn't bother him at first, but the wounds recently began pulsating and turning a dark purplish color. That wasn't the only change. At least once a day, adrenaline rushed through John's body, and his jaws clinched together. Once, it happened in front of his mom. She yelped and claimed John's eyes were yellow. He ran to the kitchen and splashed cold water on his face. His fists relaxed and his body decompressed. When he returned to the living room, the worry left Mrs. Daggon's face. John's eyes were back to normal.

> At first, I thought I was just having some side effects from the meds the doc gave me to prevent infection, but that ain't the case.

He wrote about not showing up in the candid Polaroid with Cassie. Then admitted the problem was worsening. He couldn't see his reflection in the mirror anymore.

I know it sounds bizarre, but I think I am turning into a vampire or whatever that creature was that attacked me. I thought about telling Cassie today, but I didn't want her laughing at me or even worse, running from me. I almost told Billy the night I took that photo, but I couldn't bring myself to it and ruin his night. He's staying at Shane's tonight, so I'll have to wait. But I HAVE GOT TO TELL HIM AFTER THE GAME.

***

*And we are live here for the championship game of the Annual Frisco Fall Fest Classic, where it's the Burdine Bruins taking on the Willow Springs Warriors. I'm your host Carl Ables, and I am once again joined by my cohost, Cecil Edwards. The big story of the evening is that sophomore John Daggon is available tonight, after being attacked last Saturday night by what they are calling a bat.*

*Carl, he may be cleared to play, but I don't expect him to get any minutes tonight. I'd have to assume that Coach Jenkins would give his man more time to recover and look deeper down the bench for this evening's game.*

*Well, we'll soon find out, won't we, Cecil? The crowd is piling in, and the teams are warming up for the heavyweight clash. Thank you for tuning in to 97.1, we'll be right back with the game.*

John stood at the top of the key, wearing a wife-beater

          Brock Enloe

and warm-up pants, his pants tucked into his socks. He fidgeted with the bandage on his neck, while a line of players on either side of him ran through the pregame layup drill.

Billy jogged over to his brother. "Yo," he said, "you good man?"

"I'm good," John insisted.

Billy squinted at John's face. "You're sweating, man—a lot. You sure you're okay?"

"I'm fine." John rubbed his neck and forced a smile. "Let's just win this and go home."

Billy got back in line. He rebounded another player's shot and passed it to the next guy in line. John stayed at the top of the key, rubbing his neck and sweating. Billy turned to alert the coach.

"Billy, wake up!" Coach Jenkins clapped. "Captain's meeting at half-court. Go!"

"Coach, something's wrong with John."

Coach yelled at John to get moving or get off the court. John scratched his neck, then slunk into the warm-up line. Billy made his way to half-court. Keeping his eyes locked on John, he didn't see Rachel walk in with Cassie, Shane, and Jimmy.

*Welcome back! Both teams with their starting five are out there now, and it seems you were right, Cecil. John Daggon is not starting tonight for the Bruins.*

*Well, I hate it for him and the Bruins, but I believe that's the smart move. I mean, for goodness's sake, this time last week he was being rushed to the hospital.*

Cassie pointed at the end of the bench, where John sat three feet from the next player. "I thought he was cleared to play."

"He is," Jimmy said, "by the doctor. Guess Coach Jenkins doesn't agree with the medical expert."

"Burdine has never won this tournament, and now that we're in the championship, they don't play the second-best player on the team." Shane peeled back the wrapper of a Sugar Daddy. "Perfect plan."

*And we are underway. Willow Springs winning the tip brings the ball down. A quick pass to the wing, who immediately swings it to the corner, finding an open player. The three is up, and good. Three to zero as the warriors grab the early lead.*

For two quarters, Willow Springs built a sizable lead. As the point spread increased, John felt more like himself. He was still in warm-up pants and a wife-beater, but he was focused on the game and urging his team to play harder.

*With twenty seconds left in the first half, the Bruins can cut the lead to ten here with a basket. Billy passes the ball in to Tommy, who holds the ball at the top of the key, running the time down. With now only eight seconds remaining, Tommy sweeps the ball through and drives to the basket. Four, three, two... Oh! He goes down hard and loses it out of bounds. That will do it for the first half.*

*It will, Carl, and that may do it for Tommy as well, who's still down, grabbing at his ankle.*

     Brock Enloe

"Cowards! That's what you guys are—COWARDS!" Coach Jenkins slammed his clipboard on the locker-room floor, as the door popped open.

Tommy hobbled in with the school's athletic trainer under one arm and the team manager under the other. They eased Tommy onto the locker room bench and made a quick, quiet exit.

"Listen, guys," Coach continued, "this team is not better than us! They are making you look soft and you're letting 'em do it. Wake up! And dang it, John, I wasn't going to play you tonight, but I need you. You're in for Tommy."

John nodded and caught Billy's attention, then mouthed, "Let's go!" Adrenaline pulsed through his body. He clinched his fists. Sweat trickled down his brow.

The team huddled up and stacked their hands, while John changed into his uniform. "One, two, three, Burdine!"

"John," Billy said, "I don't know about this."

John tied his shoes, then stood up to face his brother. Billy backed away. "Your eyes look crazy," Billy said, "they're almost yellow."

"The championship is ours." John clinched his jaw. "Let's go handle business."

*Well, folks, coming out of the tunnel after the half is number three, John Daggon, and—correct me if I'm wrong, Cecil, but it seems he is dressed out in his*

*Burdine High uniform, ready to play.*

   *With Tommy down, Coach must have felt they had no choice but to call on John Daggon. Let's see if the Daggon brothers can get this team going and spark a comeback here.*

Shane flirted with some random girls sitting behind him in the bleachers. The Sugar Daddy stick hung out of his mouth like a cigarette.

"Dude!" Jimmy tugged on Shane's shirttail. "Looks like he is going to play!"

Shane grabbed the candy stick from his mouth and shouted, "Here we go, John!"

   *Burdine ball coming out of half. John brings the ball up, passes to Billy, who swings it back. John pulls up for three, and it goes! Burdine down nine.*

The crowd got to their feet, chanting, "DE-FENSE, DE-FENSE!"

   *Willow Springs inbounds the ball, but it's stolen by Billy, who takes it and cashes it for a quick two. The Bruins within seven now.*

The Bruins got another stop, and John buried his second three, cutting the lead to four. Coach Jenkins pulled his players close. "Let's press up right here!" he screamed to be heard over the crowd. "They can't handle the pressure!"

   *What a different team this has been since coming out of half. Let's see if they can keep things rolling and tie this game up, Carl.*

 Brock Enloe

When the buzzer sounded at the end of the third quarter, Burdine trailed by one. John collapsed on the bench. His head rang. A sharp pain reached behind his eyes. He grabbed a water cup and splashed it on his face, then shook his head. He grabbed two more water cups and repeated the process. The pain faded, and the buzzer sounded to signal the start of the fourth quarter. John walked back out on the court.



Billy pushed off the floor, then pulled John away from the fouling defender. John yelled threats as Billy spun John toward him.

"We need you, John—don't do anything stupid. And you sure you're okay?" Billy said. "Your eyes…"

*Things are getting chippy here down the stretch. But Billy at the line for two. He misses the first one. Daggon takes a deep breath before shooting the second, and it's good. With that, we're all tied up.*

A Willow Springs player grabbed the ball, and the rest of the players scattered for the inbounds pass. But John didn't move. Not his feet at least. He stood just outside the paint, shaking his head and grabbing and pulling at his hair.

"Yo," Jimmy said to Shane, "is he okay?"

John leaned down and slapped the floor with both hands before dropping into a defensive stance.

Shane shrugged. "Yeah, dude, I'm sure he's just caught up in the intensity of the game."

*Thirty-five seconds to play, Willow Springs with a one-point lead and the ball. Burdine presses up to force a steal before resorting to foul. The Warriors try to inbound deep, but it is stolen! Burdine swings the ball ahead to John, who catches it on the wing. Sweeping the ball through and taking two dribbles, he goes up. And—Oh, man! John Daggon just went up and over the defender and threw it down! The basket counts, and the foul!*

John bounced to his feet and straddled the defender, who laid on his back. "And one."

Still on the ground, the defender shoved John with both hands. John reared back and hit the guy square in

          Brock Enloe

the jaw. The crowd let out a collective "Ooooh!" John picked the guy up and slammed him back to the ground, before pummeling him with more blows. A satisfied smile spread across John's face as he swung, and two sharp canine teeth poked out from his closed lips.

Then, John was in the air. Billy slung John over his shoulder and carried him to the locker room. He dropped him to his feet and pushed him onto a bench. "Stay here!"

When the final buzzer rang out, John was in his wife beater and warm-up pants. His breathing was calm and he felt like his old self as he heard the announcer: "Burdine High completes the comeback and wins the Fall Fest Classic for the first time in school history!"

***

For bludgeoning the guy who fouled Billy, John earned a five-game suspension. Missing the games barely registered on John's radar though. He was consumed with his symptoms, which were getting uncontrollable.

Billy stomped toward their bedroom and stopped in the doorway. John tucked his journal under his pillow.

"What is going on with you, bro?" Billy raised his arms and placed his hands on top of the doorframe.

John crossed his legs and put his hands behind his head. "Nothing, what do you mean?"

"You've been acting weird since the attack—different. You're short-tempered, you sweat like a madman, your eyes change colors, and tonight—" Billy swallowed hard. "Tonight, at the game..."

"Tonight at the game what?"

Fear oozed from Billy's eyes. "You had...fangs."

John covered his face with his hands. "I don't know what's going on. The first few days after the attack, I felt different," he said, "but it was a good different. Strong, sharp, powerful. I still feel those things, but now I have other feelings, other symptoms."

Billy listened without comment. Mostly because he didn't know what to say.

John sniffled and wiped his nose with the back of his hand. He cleared his throat and continued, "When I sweat, I feel my heart beating inside my neck, right where that thing bit me. Then I get this huge rush of adrenaline, like I can do anything, but it brings a sharp pain behind my eyes."

"And that's what happened tonight?"

"Tonight?" John sat up and cocked his head to the side. "Tonight, I got extremely hot, like I had the worst fever ever, and my head rang like a thousand alarm clocks were in there going off. I tried to control my emotions, but it was like I physically could not fight it off. That is the first time that it's been that bad."

"John, you had a crazy look when you were beating that kid, and you had giant fangs hanging out of your mouth." Billy shuddered. "Are you a vampire or something? Is that what attacked you that night?"

John said whatever attacked him, it messed him up. He handed Billy the Polaroid of him and Cassie.

"I was sitting right by her." John's eyes dropped to the floor. "Can you see me in the picture?"

Billy shook his head, then took a couple steps into the room. With his eyes locked on John, Billy grabbed the

    Brock Enloe

door handle and shut the door behind him. He peeked at the mirror screwed into the back of the door. His mirror image looked back at him. He pressed his face close to the mirror until he saw John's bed in the mirror.

Billy looked at John, then the mirror. Moved in closer to the mirror and kept looking. The mirror reflected the bed from headboard to footboard, but there was something missing. John. "Oh, dude," Billy muttered, "this isn't good."

"I know, and I'm scared, dude!" John's voice shook. He squeezed his head with his hands. "I don't want to turn into—into one of those things."

"You won't, I promise. We're gonna figure this out."

John fell back on his bed and draped an arm over his eyes.

"First things first. We got to figure out what that thing was that attacked you. Maybe Shane was right," Billy said. "Maybe it was a mountain bat."

John rolled over and pulled a piece of paper from his bookbag. "I don't think Shane is lying anymore." He handed Billy the newspaper article about mountain bats.

Billy read it and went into instructor mode. "Tomorrow, get Cassie and Jimmy to meet us at The Roost. I'll get Shane and Rachel. Between the six of us, we'll figure out what to do. For now," he said, opening their bedroom door, "try to get some sleep."

John thanked Billy, put his head on his pillow, and closed his eyes.

"Whoa there, blood sucker!" Billy knocked on the doorframe. "We're gonna fix you, but until then, you're on the couch."

"Dude, I don't even crave blood."

"Yeah, not yet." Billy yanked the pillow out from under John's head and tossed it in the hallway.

John rolled his eyes and sulked into the hallway. As he neared the living room, a light clicking sounded behind him as Billy locked the bedroom door.

# CHAPTER 5

# R&D

"Okay, can someone please tell me what's so important that I had to miss Sunday lunch?" Shane held his stomach with both hands. "My grandma makes the best fried chicken after church."

"Yeah," Jimmy added, "what's going on? This is weird!"

Billy recommended everyone sit down, then he motioned for John to take the floor. John dropped Cassie's hand and stood in front of the couch at The Roost. All eyes were on him.

"So, a week ago, I was attacked by that thing."

"Yes, we know," Shane said. "I'm missing fried chicken for this?"

John ignored the interruption. "Since then, I've been experiencing some odd symptoms. At first, I brushed 'em off, thinking it would pass, but it continued to get worse. Last night at the game was the first time I lost control."

"Oh, we know," Shane said. "We all watched you whoop that man!"

"Let him finish," Billy said sternly.

Shane raised one hand and used the other to cover his mouth.

"I thought the symptoms were just from trauma or maybe the medicine they gave me, but I don't think that's the case now."

The group shifted uneasily in their seats. Cassie tucked her hair behind her ear.

John made eye contact with Cassie and mumbled, "I think, uh...I think—"

"Dude, spit it out!" Shane hollered.

John clenched his fists. "I think I'm turning into one of those creatures."

The room went quiet, until Shane busted out laughing.

"Dude, what?" Shane got up from the couch and laughed. "This is why I missed Sunday lunch?"

"Sit down!" Billy shoved Shane back on the couch, then took a seat beside Rachel. "John, show them the picture."

John pulled the crumpled Polaroid out of his pocket slowly and handed it to Cassie. She gave the photo a double take, then looked back at John.

"I'm so confused," she said, passing the picture to Shane. "Is this why you didn't show me the picture that night?"

John rubbed his neck and watched everyone examine the photo.

"Let me get this right," Shane said, wagging the

                    Brock Enloe

picture in the air, "you want me to believe that the reason you didn't show up in this photo is because you're some type of vampire creature?"

John pulled one of his mother's old compact mirrors from his back pocket. He held it toward his friends. They smiled at their reflections. Jimmy pretended to preen himself in front of it. Billy moved to his brother's side, took the mirror from John, and closed it.

"Now, look at this," John said. He took a knee in front of the couch.

Billy reopened the compact mirror and pointed it at the group. Everyone showed up in the reflection but John. Shane and Jimmy leaned left and right, trying to find an angle that showed John's reflection.

"Now do you believe me?" John eyed his friends in the mirror. "Because I really need your help."

Billy closed the mirror and stuffed it in his pocket. "We need to know what that thing was. If we figure that out, we can hopefully find a way to save John, before— you know, he turns. Fully."

The normally boisterous group sat stunned, staring fearfully at John.

"Listen, I'm just as scared as you guys are." John's eyes softened with defeat. "I'm just asking for your help. You're the only shot I have at stopping whatever this is."

Billy patted John on the back and helped him to his feet. "You know you got me, little brother." The two hugged for a long moment, then turned to see the response of their friends.

Cassie gave John a hug. Rachel and Jimmy followed suit. Shane was the only one left on the couch.

"Well?" Billy said.

Shane threw his hands in the air. "Okay, yeah, I'm in. So, what's the plan?"

John told everyone to get back on the couch. Then he slid the coffee table in front of it and slammed down the article from the *Burdine Post*. "This mentions mountain bats." He sighed. "I printed it off the day we went to the library for our history project."

Cassie feigned anger and winked at John. "No more secrets!"

The group read the short article, then chattered back and forth about it. All the while, Jimmy sat back, chewing on his fingernails. When Billy asked if he had anything to add, Jimmy shook his head.

"You know something, Jimmy," John said. "What is it?"

Jimmy stayed quiet.

"Come on, man, stop lying." John tapped the newspaper with one finger. "Every time Shane brought up the mountain bats, you denied it and always changed the subject. You never like to stay out after dark. That day we fished on the mountain and were catching big trout with every cast, you made us leave two hours before sunset. When we took the handcar to the cave entrance, you immediately started acting different the second we got there. Not to mention, we had to BEG you to go to the bonfire party that night. I thought you were just a weirdo, but it all makes sense now. You know something."

Jimmy stared at the ground and shook his head.

"I think you had it right the first time," Shane said. "He's just a weirdo."

     Brock Enloe

"You're my best friend, dude. Please," John pleaded, "I don't want to turn into one of those things."

Jimmy's eyes were full of tears. "I can't," he said through sniffles. "My dad told me not to talk about it."

Billy grabbed Jimmy by the shoulder. "Talk about what?"

"Those things—mountain bats, whatever they are." Jimmy trembled. "Yes, I knew they were out there because my dad is over this section of the Frisco Railroad. There have been many supposed train accidents during his time with the company."

"Wait," John said, scratching at his neck, "the accident last week wasn't a train accident, but a mountain bat attack?"

Jimmy wiped at his nose and nodded. "I wanted to tell you guys, but my dad will lose his job if word gets out."

"We won't say a word," John said. "Right, guys?"

Shane, Billy, Rachel, and Cassie all agreed to keep the secret a secret. Billy asked Jimmy what to do now, how to save John.

"I'm not sure." Jimmy popped the knuckles on his hand and leaned back on the couch. "Yeah, umm, as far as we know, John is the first survivor."

The reality of the situation rested heavily on The Roost. John had been attacked by a mysterious bat creature. The creature had attacked before, but John was the first victim to survive. Now, a group of high schoolers had to find a solution.

Cassie spoke up first. "What if we go ask the ranger? He has to know what that creature is. He could help us."

"Oh, he knows," Shane said, "but he ain't helping us. I questioned him the whole way to the hospital, and he wouldn't say a word."

"Maybe he really doesn't know." Rachel offered.

"No, he definitely knows," Billy said. "He had a pistol on his hip the night of the attack."

"And?" John said. "What does that got to do with anything?"

Billy pinched his eyes closed. "Do you remember what he shot at the creature?"

"No, I'm sorry," John scoffed. "I was too busy getting mauled."

Cassie raised her hand as if she were in class, then shouted, "A flare!"

"That's right," Billy said, popping his eyes open. "Now, if you were the ranger, which would you have shot: the flare or the gun?"

Shane held up an imaginary gun and pulled the trigger. "The gun, obviously."

"My point exactly!" Billy crossed his arms. "Anyone in their right mind would've used the gun, unless—"

"Unless they knew the flare would've scared the beast off," Jimmy said, finishing Billy's thought.

"Precisely," Billy declared. "The ranger knows what that thing is."

...

The next day, John finished a journal entry as the others emerged from the woods.

We don't need the ranger, he won't tell us

        Brock Enloe

John hopped down from the loft and welcomed the crew. "Everyone got what they need?"

Everyone held up their items for inspection. John checked off the necessary tools in his head. Walkie-talkies: Check. Bag phone: Check. Crowbar: Check. Flare gun: Check.

One item was missing. John scowled at Shane. "You didn't bring the camera?"

Shane swung the camera out from behind his back. "Still don't know why we need this thing."

"Because we're taking pictures," John said, "not stuff." He then ran through the plan.

The boys would ride the handcar up the mountain. Meanwhile, Rachel and Cassie would drive The Fury, parking near the site of the attack the night of the bonfire. There, the girls would pop the hood and call the ranger for help, explaining that they broke down. Once the ranger heads out on his rescue mission, the girls would notify the boys, who would hop off the tracks and make the short walk to the ranger's abandoned hut. Billy would pry open the hut's window, and the boys would spend a few minutes looking for any helpful information.

"Dusk is at five thirty." John grimaced at his watch. "It's a fifteen-minute drive down the mountain in The Fury and a twenty-five-minute trek in the handcar. We can get back in eighteen-ish minutes if we don't use the hand brake. Be attentive of the time, we must be off the mountain before dark. We'll all meet back here at The Roost when we're done. Good luck."

*A Bat Among Bruins*      97

Shane and Jimmy began to push the handcar toward the double doors. They glanced behind them just as Cassie pulled John in for a long kiss.

"Be safe," Cassie said as their lips separated. "No matter what, get back before dark."

Billy swung open the doors and helped Shane push the handcar out of The Roost. Rachel rushed to Billy as he hopped onto the handcar. "Be careful," she said, then gave him a quick kiss.

"We have Batman with us," Shane joked. "We'll be fine."

The girls watched the handcar roll out of sight before locking the barn doors and sprinting to The Fury, which was parked behind the Daggons' house.

Rachel cranked the engine, and Cassie tuned the radio to 97.1.

*Good afternoon, Burdine! We'll get back to the music in just a moment, but first we wanted to make you aware of the bad weather rolling in within the next hour. Expect heavy rain, high winds, and thunderstorm warnings throughout the night. Stay safe and thank you for listening! Now, back to the music.*

Cassie was on the walkie-talkie before George Michael's "Faith" kicked in. "Come in," she said into the handheld device. "Can you guys hear me?"

A long, steady static answered.

"Hello," Cassie repeated. "Can you hear me?"

More static, and then, "Yeah, we got you!" It was Billy. "What's up?"

     Brock Enloe

"Radio guy just said there's bad weather rolling in within the next hour," Cassie said.

When she released the talk button, Jimmy responded on the other end. "We already started," he said. "Plus, John could be one of those things any minute. I vote we continue on."

The walkie-talkie returned to static for a moment. "Billy here again. We better make it fast. Y'all be safe, and let us know when the coast is clear."

Rachel pressed the gas pedal, and The Fury responded with a roar that sped them up the mountain. On the tracks, the boys sped past the rushing creek and through the line of pines, as storm clouds formed above the lone mountain top in the distance.

Shane tapped his wrist nervously. "I thought dusk was at five thirty," he shouted.

"Clouds are bringing night fast," Billy said.

A gust of wind sent chill bumps up John's arm. "We got to hurry."

On top of the mountain, Rachel threw The Fury in park, and killed the engine. Cassie hustled out to prop open the hood, while Rachel called the ranger hut with her dad's bag phone.

Cassie leaned against the side of The Fury as Rachel hung up the phone.

"No answer," Rachel said.

"Call it again," Cassie said. "We need him or the whole night is a waste."

Rachel punched in the ranger's phone number, as the first rain drops made their mark on The Fury's dirty paint job. Rachel listened as the phone rang five times.

"Come in, come in!" Cassie shouted into the walkie-talkie.

"Are we good to go?" Billy asked.

"No one picked up," Cassie said.

"The ranger didn't answer?" Billy gathered his thoughts with his thumb on the talk button. "Alright, well, we're moving in. Keep trying the number, and let us know if you get through."

John locked the brake on the handcar, grabbed his bag, and led the boys toward the hut. Rain drizzled down as they passed through the woods, and a dense fog settled between the trees.

"This way," John said, pointing toward the hut that was nearly hidden by the fog. "Check with the girls."

Billy clicked the radio on quietly. "We have the hut in sight. Did the ranger ever answer?"

"Yes, he said he'd be here in fifteen minutes. That was 5 minutes ago," Cassie said. "Coast should be clear."

"Let's move." John crouched and moved soundlessly toward the hut. The others followed his lead, as the rain picked up. When they reached the ranger's hut, the rain splattered against the roof, muffling their whispers.

"You're up." John stepped to the side.

Billy slid the crowbar into place and popped the window open. Behind him, the forest was covered in a blanket of white fog. John pulled a flashlight from his bag and maneuvered through the window. A moment later, the front door popped open.

"Ten minutes or less," he whispered. "Billy and I will check the left wing. Jimmy and Shane, y'all check the right."

Billy and John scoured the hut for hints or clues or anything useful. They found nothing, so they worked their way back toward the front entrance. When they turned the corner, Shane called out. He'd found something.

Billy and John rushed toward Shane and Jimmy. The light from their flashlights bounced down the hallway, where Shane and Jimmy held up handfuls of paper. Then, they stopped in their tracks.

"Every one of these talks about the bat things!" Jimmy said, holding up papers in both hands. "They're real, and there are stacks of papers that talk about them on this desk!"

"Come look, guys," Shane said. "It's crazy."

Billy and John didn't reply. They stood still, frozen in place, gawking at the ceiling above their friends.

"What's your deal?" Shane rustled the papers toward Billy and John. "You've got to—"

John held a finger over his mouth and tiptoed toward Shane. Billy pointed at the ceiling.

Shane looked up and stifled the start of a scream. Overhead, a bat-like creature hung upside down from the hut's wooden ceiling beams. Its leathery wings surrounded its body as it slept, its body expanding and contracting with every breath.

John reached toward a stack of papers, but his shaky hands knocked the papers onto the floor behind the desk.

"Shoot," he mumbled, then lowered himself to his knees to pick up the papers.

As Shane walked around the desk to help grab the papers, John came face to face with the ranger. But the ranger wasn't hiding. He wasn't even alive. His body was ripped to shreds, and the floor around him was stained with days-old blood.

Shane stood behind him and stifled another scream.

"Radio the girls," John whispered to Billy. "Tell them to abort."

"Why?" Billy questioned.

"Tell them to abort," John repeated, "now!"

John reached over the corpse and grabbed the papers. He shoved them into his bag and shuffled out from under the desk. As he got to his feet, a light flashed.

Shane held his camera toward the ranger's lifeless body and gave a thumbs-up.

"Dude, you idiot!" John grabbed Shane's shoulder and dragged him to his feet. "The flash!"

The pair scrambled toward the door as a loud crack of thunder sounded outside.

"Run!" John pushed the others through the door and into the thick fog. He gave one last look up, where the creature began to awaken, then slammed the door shut behind him.

Ahead, Billy shouted into the walkie-talkie: "Abort! Abort!"

John caught up to him and snatched the walkie-talkie from him. "Cassie, Rachel, abort—the ranger is dead!"

Lightning lit up the woods, guiding the boys toward the train tracks.

"Dead?" Rachel asked over the walkie. "He's walking up to the car right now."

"Please believe me," John shouted. "Whatever that is, it's not the ranger! Abort! Get back to The Roost, now! There's no time to explain."

Behind them, the creature screeched inside the hut. The boys stumbled through the forest, searching for the way back to the handcar. Thunder shook the ground, but any lightning that struck didn't cut through the fog.

"I can't see nothing!" Jimmy screamed, as the creature screeched again, filling the dense fog with terror.

"This way!" Billy yelled.

The boys crawled on all fours, using the fog to hide them from the creature. When they finally navigated their way to the handcar, John and Billy took the pedaling seats, while Shane and Jimmy hopped on the back. John released the park brake and started pedaling. Shane and Jimmy clung to the handcar and tried to see into the impenetrable fog behind them.

The rain eased to a mist, but the skies were pitch black. John pedaled with everything in him and handed Jimmy the flare gun from his bag. "If you see the creature," he said, "fire away!"

The creature screeched again, its echo so close, so loud, it rattled the small handcar.

John grabbed the walkie from Billy. "We got company! We need you guys at The Roost with the barn doors open. We're going to come in at full speed. Just close the doors as soon as we're in."

Cassie slammed the talk button down. "What's going on!"

"Just have the barn doors open and be ready!" John handed the walkie to Shane, then released the brake altogether. The handcar picked up speed immediately. "Alright boys, HOLD ON!"

The handcar raced down the mountain, weaving

and wobbling on the tracks, dropping in elevation and submerging beneath the fog. An angry screech called through the fog.

"We're almost to the turnoff!" John pulled the handbrake slightly, slowing the handcar enough to guide it toward the runoff bit of track that led to The Roost.

A bright light lit up the sky, as a flare whistled away behind them. John and Billy ducked.

"Shoot, I missed!" Jimmy yelled.

Now, all four had their backs to their destination and their eyes on the tracks behind.

"There he is!" Billy said.

The creature cut through the fog above and dove toward the handcar.

"Shoot it!" Billy, Shane, and John shouted.

The night lit up and then darkened again. "I hit it!" Jimmy cried.

The creature vanished into the fog as the depot came into sight. Billy and John pedaled furiously as the girls stood by, ready to close the doors behind them. The handcar zipped into The Roost, and the handbrake screamed as John pulled it with his entire body weight. Just at the end of the track, the handcar came to a stop. The girls slammed and locked the doors, as the boys hurried to the fogged-up window to peer into the darkness.

John panted and dropped to the floor. "I think we're clear."

Rachel squatted in front of John. "What happened up there?"

"The ranger is dead," John said, taking off his rain-soaked jacket.

     Brock Enloe

"But we saw the ranger," Cassie said. "I mean, we talked to him on the phone at least."

"Whoever you saw, whoever you talked with...it wasn't the ranger." Shane walked in circles around the group that was sitting around John.

"We got a picture," John said. "Right, Shane?"

Shane raised a thin, black camera. "Yeah, but it will need time to develop."

"We don't have time for pictures," Cassie said. "That creature knows where we are. Won't it come back?"

A dog howled outside. Jimmy jumped.

"I don't know," Billy said, "but I do know that no one leaves The Roost until morning. We're all sleeping here. Go ahead and use Rachel's bag phone to call home. Don't need our families going out in the dark looking for us."

Rachel called her parents first, then the rest followed suit. Afterward, John whipped his bag off his back and pulled out the papers taken from the ranger's hut. The group probed every page, until the excitement of the day wore off. John offered to take the first watch. He still had a lot of thinking to do.

With Cassie snoozing beside him, John used his journal to document what he learned from the stolen papers.

"Mountain bat" was just what the townspeople call it. The Native Americans referred to the creature as a "stryx," "strigoi" for plural.

They described it as this bird of ill omen, a vampire-like creature. They're nocturnal creatures that feast on human blood and flesh.

These creatures can see perfectly in the

dark, they sense life forces and are drawn to them. The natives believed that they could even communicate and summon other strigoi with their screeches.

Unlike vampires, strigoi have the ability to transform and shape shift, often taking the form of prior victims to lure others in to their doom. This explains how the girls saw the ranger, even though he was dead.

Some say there are hundreds of strigoi in the mountain, but who knows.

We can confirm that there are at least two, because one was in the hut with us and the other was disguised as the ranger and trying to lure the girls.

That is all the information we found. No explanation on where these creatures came from, how long a victim has until they fully turn, or how to cure a victim who has been bit.

Our best chance is to research the Native's folklore even further. The Native Museum in Newburg, Missouri, isn't open anymore, but Jimmy said Newburg hosts an annual fall festival. Every year, there are several booths and tents set up there that honor the Native culture. He says they sell dream catchers and other Native American items. They may be able to help us. It's a long shot, but we're out of options.

John put his pen down and leaned against the wall, wondering why he didn't feel sleepy. Was it fear or his unnatural transition into becoming nocturnal?

# CHAPTER 6

# HORTICULTURE

For four days after the ranger-hut operation, the crew searched the library for more information on strigoi. Day after day, they came up empty-handed. And day after day, John's symptoms occurred more frequently. He put a lot of hope in finding answers at the fall festival. He planned to get there when it opened at one. It meant skipping school and the game, but his life was on the line. Besides, he couldn't play basketball for five more games.

He tried getting somebody to join him, but they all declined. Billy had the upcoming game, and he had to be at school to play. Shane had a math test during last period, and Jimmy planned on skipping school, but his parents caught wind and put an abrupt end to his plan. Rachel was going to Billy's game, and Cassie had to work. Not that Cassie would join John anyway. As he wrote in his journal,

She isn't the type to skip school.

John dropped down from the loft and landed on his feet like a superhero. He double-checked his bookbag—"Flashlight, walkie, flare"—before throwing it on the handcar. He began wheeling the handcar out of The Roost when his throat caught. Someone was knocking on the front door.

He slowly approached the door, as the handle turned and the door opened.

"Let me in, silly!" Cassie chuckled and patted John on the chest as she walked into The Roost.

John stepped back, confused. "What are you doing here?"

"*We* are going to the fall festival," Cassie said. "Together."

"I thought you had school and work," John said.

"Well," she said with a wink, "the cute boy in my history class got suspended and won't be there, so I figured it would be a good day to skip."

"And work?"

"I called in sick." She faked a cough. "Now, it's my turn to ask the questions. What are you doing out here?"

John rested one foot on the handcar. "I've been sleeping out here."

"But why?"

"Because I'm a vampire, remember? Don't want to lose control and go all Dracula on my family."

Cassie held her arms out toward John. "That makes me sad, you out here sleeping all alone. When are you gonna move back to your house?"

"When we break this curse, I guess." John pushed the handcar out of The Roost. "Enough questions. Ready?"



Brock Enloe

Cassie climbed onto the handcar and smiled. The two followed the map as the tracks led them through a fall-stained forest, surrounded by the sounds of rustling leaves and chirping birds. A cool, crisp breeze blew through their hair. The handcar clicked over the tracks.

The trip took longer than expected, but neither complained. Eventually, they arrived on the outskirts of Newburg, Missouri. John closed the map and parked the handcar out of sight. Following the smell of pumpkin pie, funnel cake, and popcorn, the two made their way toward the festival.

"Find the tents Jimmy referred to and get the information we need," John said. "Then we can get some funnel cake."

Cassie licked her lips at the thought.

At the gate, John and Cassie realized this was no ordinary festival. There were multiple roller coasters, a petting zoo, carnival games, food trucks, and even live music with a dance floor.

Cassie let out a schoolgirl squeal, and John squeezed her hand tight. The two wandered the fairgrounds, until Cassie saw a Native American tent. She pointed toward a booth selling dream catchers. It was just like Jimmy said.

John cut through a thin crowd of people going in every direction and approached the tent. A middle-aged Native woman stood inside the tent. Wisps of white highlighted her dark, long hair.

"How can I help you?" she asked.

John didn't want to scare her away, so he asked for some history on Native culture. The Native woman obliged with a brief discussion of the local tribes and how dream catchers fit into their culture. As she spoke, John tapped his foot quickly. When she finished, John couldn't hold back any longer.

"Listen," he said, scratching his neck, "I know this is a random thing to ask, but what can you tell me about strigoi?"

Cassie pressed against John's side. He wrapped an arm around her as the color drained from the Native woman's face.

"No dream catcher." The Native woman's lip quivered. "Leave."

"Oh, I'll buy one." John jammed his hands in his jeans pocket for cash. "Please, I just need to know about those creatures. I mean, I want to know about those, um, legends."

The Native woman shook her head and repeated, "Leave."

John kept digging his hands in his pockets and scanned the area behind him. No one passing by seemed interested in his conversation. He leaned over the fold-up table covered in dream catchers and pulled down his hoodie.

"Please," he begged, showing the bite marks on his neck, "I need help."

The Native woman murmured something in a language John didn't understand, then she locked her register and flipped the Open sign to Closed. She pointed toward a small, black tent. "Over there," she said.

"What do you mean?" Cassie asked.

"Help. Over there."

John considered the black tent, then turned back for

clarification. But the Native woman was gone. Cassie and John rushed to the tent. A sign that read MEDICINE MAN hung askew, taped to the top of the tent canvas.

"Well?" John said, looking at Cassie. She shrugged.

John lifted the black curtain and walked in. Cassie grabbed the tail of John's shirt and followed.

Inside the tent, a sliver of light cut through the darkness. Cassie held up a piece of paper from the table in the light.

"You're early," Cassie read. "Medicine man will be here at six."

"Six?" John slammed a hand against the table. "That's too late. Even if we get answers right away, we have a two-hour trek home. I can't risk you being out after dark."

Cassie set the sign back on the table. "This is our only option, and we don't know how much time you have."

John rubbed the two raised dots on his neck. "We'll leave right after, okay? I mean, we are far from the mountain, so we should be alright."

The two exited the tent and watched the growing number of fairgoers mill about.

"So, where to first?" John asked.

A couple minutes later, Cassie held a bright-pink shock of cotton candy. Her dad used to bring her to the fall festival every year, and they always grabbed cotton candy before doing anything else. It was the same vendor every year, and surprisingly, he was still at it.

"And this is not just any cotton candy," she insisted. "It's the best cotton candy in the world!"

John wiped a piece of pink fluff from Cassie's mouth and licked it off his finger. "Not bad," he admitted. "And

I've never heard you talk about your dad before."

"Yeah." Cassie fidgeted with her cone of cotton candy. "He was the best."

He *was* the best. Past tense. John sat in awkward silence, debating whether to dig deeper. Before he could, Cassie answered his unasked question. "He passed two years ago. Car accident."

"I'm so sorry." John enveloped Cassie's hand in his.

"Thank you," she said, pain filling her eyes. "Thank you for the cotton candy."

An oversized clock hanging from a nearby vendor tent read three forty-eight. They had two more hours and some change before the medicine man arrived.

"So," Cassie said, willing a smile across her face, "what's next on the fun agenda?"

The next couple hours were spent screaming on Pharaoh's Phury, snuggling on the Ferris wheel, and getting ripped off by rigged carnival games. The sun began to set.

"Time to go see the medicine man," Cassie said.

"Not quite," John said. "There's one more thing we got to do."

He led Cassie to the black-and-white checkered dance floor and wrapped his arms around Cassie's waist as a live band started "I Think They Call This Love." Cassie rested her hands on John's shoulders, as their bodies swayed to the rhythm.

The cold fall night faded away as their bodies radiated warmth. They gazed into one another's eyes. For a moment, everything was perfect. Then, the final note rang out, and the moment ended.

Cassie dropped her hands to her side and began to leave the dance floor, but John stopped her. Placing his hand on her face, he spoke in a soft, low voice. "No matter what we find out, no matter what happens, I just wanted to say…" The band eased into the next number. "If this turns out to be our last date, I just want you to know that it was perfect." John opened his eyes wide to keep the tears from falling. "You're all I need, and if this is how I spend my last few days, I'm okay with that."

A tear rolled down Cassie's face. She let it go. "I love you."

John lifted Cassie's chin. "I love you, too."

The two kissed under the colorful festival lights, as the band played on. Eventually, the kiss came to an end.

"Time to go," John said.

A dark-complexioned man in a tribal outfit welcomed them inside the tent. Two electric lanterns hung from the tent on either side of the medicine man, giving the room a soft glow. "Hau! How can I help you?"

John hesitated. "We were hoping you could give us some information."

The medicine man encouraged John to ask for whatever he needed. "I won't bite," he promised.

John swallowed hard, taken aback by the accidental wordplay—if it was accidental. "I need to know about stryx or strigoi."

The medicine man stood upright and took a deep breath, then reached under the table and pulled out a small leaf. Whispering a few words, he rubbed the leaf on Cassie's forehead. Nothing happened. He repeated this with John. John's eyes yellowed instantly, and a sharp pain rushed through his head. The man yelped and splashed water on John's face.

"Show me the bite," he instructed.

John pulled his hoodie to the side and turned to show the bite marks in the faint light.

"Not many survive a stryx attack." The medicine man flipped open a book on the table and held the pages open toward John and Cassie. "Once bitten, the victim has four weeks before they turn. Judging by the bite mark on your neck, you have about two weeks before you fully turn and crave blood."

John lifted his eyes from the page to the medicine man. "How do I stop it?"

"There is a flower, the Malus flower, that can help; however, it won't cure you completely. This will only alleviate the symptoms," the medicine man explained, "and push back the process by roughly four months."

"I'll take what I can get." John repositioned his hoodie to cover his neck. "Where do I get this flower?"

"Inside the mountain."

"Inside the—" John wrung his hands. "I can't get inside that!"

"Wait," Cassie said, "what mountain?"

"*The* mountain, Cassie!" John's pulse sped up, and his fist clenched. He focused on his breath and swallowed down the adrenaline spike.

"Yes, *the* mountain," the medicine man stated. "The one the Frisco Rail Company took from my people."

"I saw shadows there. I got attacked near that mountain," John cried. "Going in there is a death sentence!"

         Brock Enloe

The medicine man flipped the pages of the open book aimlessly. "Maybe so, but not going in is also a death sentence. Is it not?"

Cassie squeezed John's arm. "John," she started.

"How do we protect ourselves?" John stared at the medicine man. "If we have to go in, how do we protect ourselves from those things?"

"They are similar to vampires in many ways." The medicine man pointed at the book. His finger rested on a list.

- *Wooden stakes*
- *Garlic*
- *Holy water*
- *Sunlight*

"Bright lights will repel them temporarily," the medicine man explained, "but as soon as the light dims, the creatures will return."

John thanked the medicine man and turned to leave. "Wait!"

The medicine man handed John a picture of the Malus flower and whispered in his ear.

"What did he say?" Cassie asked when they exited the tent.

"Something about the flower and how to make herbal tea with it."

"You're acting funny, John. What did he say?"

"That's it, promise." John pulled Cassie into the thick crowd. "He gave me the heebie-jeebies."

The couple grabbed a bite to eat and headed to the handcar, hands full of trinkets won earlier in the day. John flipped on the handcar's headlight, and he and

Cassie pedaled into the darkness.

Half a mile in, the track brought them out of the woods to a long, straight stretch between two open fields. John killed the headlight as the stars lit up the night.

"This ain't so scary," John said. "It's actually kind of nice, isn't it?"

Cassie rubbed her arms. "Except for the cold."

"Here, take this." John removed his hoodie.

"Oh, I like this!" Cassie slipped the grey Burdine Basketball hoodie on. "It even smells like you."

John pedaled faster, thankful the night was dark enough to hide his blushing cheeks.

"I don't want to jinx it," Cassie said, resting her head on John's shoulder, "but if we make it back safe to The Roost, I think this will officially be the best date ever."

***

The headlight bobbed up and down with every bump of the track. Patchy fog cast villainous shadows in the woods as they passed over the small creek. John reached into his bag for the flare gun as they turned the last bend. Ahead, the headlight painted a jagged outline of something on the tracks between them and The Roost.

John brought the handcar to a slow halt and pressed the handle of the flare gun deep into his palm.

Cassie reached for John. "You think it's one of those things?"

John squinted into the darkness and aimed the flare gun at the outlined figure. "As soon as I shoot, we pedal as fast as possible."

Cassie whimpered.

"Three, two—"

The shadowed figure raised its head and screeched.

"One!" John pulled the trigger, spraying the forest with red light. He and Cassie pedaled feverishly toward the winged creature, which soared above them, screeching toward the darkness.

Inside The Roost, John yanked the handbrake and closed the barn doors.

"Can it get in?" Cassie asked nervously.

"No, I don't think so." John locked the barn doors. "The medicine man said they're like vampires. According to the movies, vampires have to be invited in."

Cassie stumbled across The Roost and took a seat on the edge of the couch. After looking out the window for a few minutes, John did the same.

"Best date ever, huh?"

"Yep." Cassie let out a sigh of relief and curled up against John.

"Looks like we're having a sleepover," John joked.

"And somehow, the best date gets even better."

John wrapped his arms around Cassie and held her tight, letting the stress of the night fade into the dark night.

"Yo! You there, John? Come in, dude!"

The stress returned. John grabbed the walkie-talkie off the coffee table. "Yo, I'm here!"

"About time," Jimmy shouted through the walkie. "We been trying to get you for an hour."

"Sorry," John said. "Just got back. Things didn't go as planned."

Cassie giggled.

"Yo," Shane called through the walkie, "who's that I hear with you?"

"Hi, guys—it's me, Cassie."

"Cassie?" Shane shouted.

"Yeah, she went with me," John said, "and that creature was waiting on us when we got back. Thankfully, we got past it, and we got what we needed."

John relayed what they learned: strigoi were like vampires, he had two weeks until he turned into one of them, and the cure was tucked away behind the boarded-up mountain. He released the talk button to a long period of static.

Cassie cocked her head toward the walkie to pick up anything the others said. But they didn't say anything. John hovered his thumb over the talk button when Billy cut in.

"Well," he said, "looks like we're cave exploring over fall break."

Jimmy said his dad had an old map of the route through the mountain, but he'd never let them have it. They made a loose plan to steal it, then agreed to meet at The Roost first thing the next morning.

"Bring as many crosses as you can find—garlic, too," John said. "The Roost is due for some redecorating."

"But the last day of school before fall break is tomorrow," Jimmy whined.

"Looks like fall break starts early this year," John replied through the walkie. "See you guys in the morning. You too, Jimmy."

John pinched the volume button to spin the walkie-talkie off but stopped. "One last thing."

"Yeah?" Jimmy replied.

"Billy, did y'all win tonight?"

Billy sighed into the walkie. "Nah, we lost by two. But we got bigger issues to handle right now."

***

"Knock, knock, love birds!" Shane thumped on The Roost's front door.

Cassie lifted her head off John's chest and peeped down from the loft bed to see Shane and Jimmy smashing their faces against the window.

"Yo," Jimmy called, "let us in, bro."

John clumsily descended the loft ladder and unlocked the door.

Shane raised an eyebrow at John. "Long night?"

"Oh, shut up, dude, I can't sleep anymore. I'm kind of nocturnal now." John yawned and looked at his watch. It was barely seven thirty. "Where's Billy?"

"He went to get Rachel," Shane explained. "Said he would be right—"

"Here!" Billy tossed a brown bag at John. "Got you and Cassie breakfast. Figured you would be hungry."

Cassie climbed down from the loft and settled down on the couch beside John. She looked like she just had the best sleep of her life. Every hair was in place, and her makeup was spot-on.

"John?" she said. "You gonna eat something or just stare at me all morning?"

John mumbled something and shoved a biscuit in his

mouth. As he ate, he gave every detail about what the medicine man said.

"So, you just eat this flower and you're all better?" Rachel eyed the photo from the medicine man.

"He said to make it into tea and drink it. The symptoms won't go away forever," John said, "but it'll buy me four more months."

"Let me get this straight." Shane was on his feet. "We're going into a boarded-up cave filled with psychotic bat creatures in the off chance we'll find a flower that will cure you for a few months. Tell me I'm missing something."

"I'm not asking you to go in the cave for me." John took the picture of the flower from Rachel. "I'm asking you to help me get the map from Mr. Bardot's office. I'm going in the cave alone."

Billy deliberated on John's idea, looking for a way out, some other remedy. As he wracked his brain, he noticed John's left eye twitch. Soon as he saw it, Billy knew John was holding something back. It was John's tell, the reason their parents always knew when John was lying.

"Alright," Billy said, "so how do we get this map?"

The map was at the Frisco Rail headquarters, inside Mr. Bardot's office. Fortunately, Jimmy's dad was a workaholic. He spent so much time at Railroad headquarters that Jimmy's mom used to think he was having an affair. So, they could go there anytime they wanted to visit him and it wouldn't seem odd. But the map was inside a giant frame. Getting it out of the office unseen wasn't going to be easy. Returning it before anyone noticed would be even harder. It would take some

     Brock Enloe

fancy footwork and a switcheroo, but it just might work.

With the plan in place, John asked the guys to vampire-proof The Roost.

"Stryx-proof," Shane corrected.

"Whatever, you know what I mean." John chewed on his last biscuit and headed toward the door. "Crosses, garlic, whatever else you guys can find that will keep them things away—bring it!"

"And where are you going?" Shane asked.

"To shower! Oh…" John rubbed his neck. "You can come with me, Cassie, and shower first."

***

The Fury rumbled up to Frisco Railroad headquarters, and Billy, Jimmy, and John piled out. A few minutes later, Mr. Bardot laughed it up at Billy's expense.

"It's not a problem at all," he said, getting up from his desk. "I've certainly had my share of car problems. Let's go see what the problem is. Think John can find his way to us when he's done in my private bathroom?"

Billy assured Mr. Bardot that John was likely bright enough. Mr. Bardot liked the joke and led the way to the parking lot. Billy cracked jokes by Mr. Bardot's side, while Jimmy pulled his office door closed.

John counted to three, then cracked the bathroom door open and slunk into Mr. Bardot's office. He lowered the framed map and flipped it over on Mr. Bardot's desk. The backside of the map was secured with flathead screws. John rifled through the desk for a screwdriver. Finding nothing in the large side drawers, he pulled open the long, thin drawer in the middle. A black-and-yellow handled screwdriver lay on top of a manila folder. He grabbed the screwdriver and uncovered the name on the file underneath: *Mentz*. His heart leapt into his throat, and he knelt down to inspect the file.

> *James Mentz*
> *615 Riverbend Drive*
> *Contract expired 1986*

"No way."

The front office door slammed shut. John tucked the file in the back of his pants and quietly closed the drawer. Billy, Jimmy, and Mr. Bardot started down the long hallway.

John twisted the screwdriver and removed three screws. The fourth wouldn't budge. "Shoot, shoot, shoot!"

John heard Billy's laugh, which was louder than usual and full of unspoken warning. The fourth screw gave. John snatched the map from the frame and replaced it with the map they found in The Roost. He got three screws in before the door cracked open.

"What are you doing?" Mr. Bardot shouted.

John was caught red-handed. He held the frame against the wall. "Uh," he started, flustered. "I came out of the bathroom and didn't know where you guys went, and I almost knocked this off the wall. I'm sorry."

"Ahh, well, thank you for catching it. That is the only map that remains of the tunnel system through the old mountain," Mr. Bardot said.

"Yeah, Dad. John, you about ready to go?" A bead of sweat lined Jimmy's upper lip.

               Brock Enloe

"Yeah," John said, backing away from the framed map. "Thanks for letting me use your facilities, Mr. Bardot. Fair warning: You may not want to go in there for a little while."

Jimmy told his dad he was staying the night at the Daggons' place.

"Have fun," Mr. Bardot said. "And boys, before you go—"

Billy, John, and Jimmy held their breath. This was it. They were busted. Mr. Bardot knew about the map.

"I wouldn't put John here in navigation." Mr. Bardot winked. "Couldn't even find his way out of my office."

Billy let out a high, nervous laugh.

As Billy put the Frisco Railway headquarters in The Fury's rearview mirror, John tossed the manila folder on the floorboard. Then he propped his left leg on the dashboard and pulled out the only known map that led to the Malus flower.

# CHAPTER 7

# CARTOGRAPHY

Darkness fell around The Roost, where everyone gathered with snacks, blankets, flashlights, and sleeping bags.

"Yo, bring me a Fruit Roll-Up when you come over here," Billy shouted.

Shane grabbed two slices of pizza with one hand and tossed a Fruit Roll-Up to Billy.

Jimmy spread the map out on the coffee table. "Alright," he said, "let's take a look at this."

The teens hovered over the map, as Shane tore a bite off his double-decker pizza.

"I'm no expert," John said, "but it looks like there are only two entrances."

Jimmy agreed. The only ways in and out were the boarded-up entrance above the iron bridge and the entrance on the other side of the mountain.

"Where's that, the other entrance?" Billy asked.

Jimmy studied the map and chewed on a fingernail. "Hard to tell, but looks like it ain't far from Willow Springs."

Shane put his fingers on the map to measure the distance, but Jimmy slapped his hand away.

"Dude, your fingers are greasy!" Jimmy shouted.

Shane scoffed, then licked his fingers. "There," he said, picking up the map, "happy now?" He walked his fingers along the map to the entrance on the far side of the mountain. "Looks like it's probably a two- to three-mile hike up the mountain."

"What are these little lines?" Rachel pointed at a series of thin lines on the map.

John spun the map to face him. "The legend says those are The Narrows. Whatever that is."

"The Narrows?" Jimmy ran a finger along the thin lines. "Those are small run-offs that let water pass through. They prevent flooding inside the mountain."

They decided to try the entrance above the iron bridge first. It was closer, and they'd at least seen it before. When Shane asked where the flower was inside the mountain, The Roost went quiet. Shane picked at his teeth and waited for an answer.

"Not sure," John said, "but you aren't going in to look, so what's it matter?"

"Oh, whatever dude. You know I ain't letting you in there alone."

Jimmy and Billy said the same.

"Awww, how sweet!" Rachel made puppy-dog eyes at the boys.

"Alright, there you have it." John pulled the map

from the coffee table and folded it up. "We ride to the boarded entrance tomorrow morning."

"Until then, let's enjoy tonight!" Billy leapt off the couch and grabbed another slice of pizza.

The next few hours consisted of board games, darts, music, and shooting the bull. Finally, everyone passed out asleep, except John. He grabbed his journal and wrote, admitting he was holding back information given by the medicine man. He even spilled the beans on the folder he snuck out of Mr. Bardot's office.

> I couldn't help myself. The outside said James Mentz—Cassie's dad! Inside mentioned a contract expiration, which I thought was odd. But then I remembered Jimmy confessing that the Frisco company hid things in the past.
>
> The file stated that Cassie's dad was killed in a car accident. He was driving a work truck to the rail yard on the other side of the mountain one night, and he never made it. Official report was that he clipped a deer, slid off the road into a tree, and somehow wound up 50 yards from the car. That's where the police report ended, but the railroad file didn't stop there. It told what happened after he struck the tree.
>
> Supposedly Mr. Mentz regained consciousness and called the rail yard, but no one answered. So, he left a message before wandering from the car for help. That's when he came across one of those creatures.
>
> I know Jimmy's dad would lose his job if these cases got released, but Cassie deserves to know

        Brock Enloe

the truth. I just don't know how to tell her, or when to tell her. Truthfully, I don't even know if Jimmy knows that Cassie's dad was one of the victims.

All I know is that we need to find this flower and then we can sort out the other issues. Ideally, the flower isn't too far inside, so we can grab it and leave, but nothing has gone according to plan thus far.

I'm trying to be optimistic though, and we are one step closer to a cure...

***

A few minutes before seven, John nudged Jimmy awake. They needed to grab some things before heading to the mountain, but first—breakfast.

The two leaned on the counter at The Marathon. Jimmy got the breakfast platter. John ordered two bacon, egg, and cheese biscuits and a coffee.

"Coffee?" Jimmy screwed up his face.

"I need something to keep me awake." The waitress set a coffee mug in front of John. He took a sip and convulsed. "Man, that is so bad, but I have to have it. The nocturnal symptoms are worsening."

"You won't have to drink that much longer," Jimmy promised. "We'll find that flower real soon."

John thanked Jimmy for his kindness and took another sip of coffee. Then another. It didn't taste any better, but John needed it to steel his courage. It was confession time.

"Jimmy, I've got something to tell you."

"Yeah, what's up?"

"When I was taking the map from your dad's office, I needed a screwdriver to open the frame, so I checked all the drawers in your dad's desk." John blew on his steaming coffee and removed a manila folder from his backpack. "Well, I found this."

Jimmy peeked inside the folder.

"Did you know?" John asked.

Jimmy slid the file back to John and gave a simple head nod.

"Alright, here you go, boys." The waitress set their plates down and smiled.

John returned the folder to his backpack. John and Jimmy picked at their food and looked everywhere except at one another.

"I know your dad will be in trouble if this gets out," John said in a low voice, "but I have to tell her."

"No, no, no!" Jimmy pleaded. "Why do you need to tell her anything?"

"Because, man."

"Because why? It won't change anything. He's dead."

John sipped on his coffee. The conversation was so painful, the bad flavor didn't affect him. "Because she deserves to know what happened," he said. "And I love her."

Jimmy dropped his fork. "Oh, you love her? Y'all have been dating for what, a month? Come on!"

"Dude, I know how it sounds, but I mean it." John fiddled with his biscuit. "With only two weeks left to live, it became clear to me."

Jimmy picked his fork up and shoved a bite of eggs into his mouth. "So, it's just screw me, right?"

"No dude, we'll figu—"

"You think I didn't want to tell you guys about this from the beginning? You're my best friend too, man! You think it's easy holding this from you? I just couldn't say anything. I can't risk getting my dad fired. Mom is sick with cancer and needs her meds." Jimmy's shoulders slumped. "They aren't cheap, you know."

John dropped his half-eaten biscuit and sipped on his black, bitter coffee. "Alright, I won't say anything."

"I'm sorry, John."

"Yeah. Me too, man."

Before they left, John ordered four more bacon, egg, and cheese biscuits to go. "Now to the hardware store," he told Jimmy. "We need some wooden stakes."

***

The Roost was asleep when John and Jimmy returned.

"Breakfast time!" Jimmy dropped the bag of biscuits on the coffee table.

"Once everyone is done with breakfast and ready," John said, as the girls made their way down from the loft, "we can head up the mountain."

Ten minutes later, the biscuits were gone, and Billy and John sat on the handcar, their feet positioned and ready to pedal away. Jimmy and Shane held onto the back of the handcar, and the girls sat on the front. John's backpack bulged with a crowbar, wooden stakes, flashlights, garlic, a flare gun, flare sticks, and water.

"Well," Shane laughed, "you definitely got everything."

"Yep." John patted his backpack. "Including the map."

As the handcar began to move, sunlight broke through the tree line. It felt like an ordinary day.

At the first turn, the handcar began picking up speed. Rachel twisted to face John and Billy. "This thing rides better than The Fury," she joked.

"Real funny," Billy said.

Soon, the joking and teasing was replaced with unease. Billy turned on the handcar's engine, as they climbed higher in elevation. What seemed like a long, lazy trip in carefree days passed in the blink of an eye, and the iron bridge appeared in record time. They glided on the track above the river, gazing at the town below, wishing they were there instead of on top of the bridge.

"We are almost there," John stated, swallowing the fear climbing up his throat.

The handcar weaved around a long curve to reveal the boarded entrance. Six hearts beat in rapid succession at the sight. John grabbed the parking brake with clammy hands and brought the handcar to a squeaky halt.

"We're here," he stuttered.

Billy grabbed the crowbar and followed John to the entrance. The others stayed on the handcar as Billy began to pry boards from the cave wall.

"How many strigoi do you think are in there?" Jimmy asked with a shaky voice.

"No telling," John said, "but they should be asleep right now."

The last nail fell out of the wood and clinked off the track rail, letting the last wooden board hit the ground. John kicked it away.

"I'm going to say this one last time," John said over his shoulder, "no one has to go in with me. I understand if you don't want to, and I won't think any less of y'all."

Shane got down slowly from the handcar and slung John's backpack over his shoulder. "Shut up, dude. We're going in with you."

The remaining members of the crew walked lightly to the mountain entrance. Standing with their flashlights cutting through the darkness, they stared into the cave.

"After you, little brother," Billy said.

John took his first timid steps into the darkness. The others trailed behind, the temperature dropping as a cool wind bellowed up from within the cave. Darkness swallowed the small beams of light from their flashlights. Water dripped from stalagmites above, sending out delicate echoes through the cave. As they made their way deeper into the mountain, the air became heavy with must and decay.

Shane held his nose and whispered, "It stinks so bad in here." He waved his flashlight, painting the cave wall in pale yellow light. As he did, something jumped off the wall.

Rachel squealed and jumped backward, nearly knocking Jimmy to the ground.

Jimmy shushed her. "It's just a cricket."

"You okay?" Billy swatted Rachel's shoulders and checked her clothing for other bugs. "Yeah, you're fine. You're fine. It's gone." He turned back toward John and faced three flashlights pointed directly at him. "Get those lights out of my face!" He raised his arm to block the light from his eyes.

"What was that?" Cassie asked.

Something rustled in the darkness ahead. The group turned as a single unit and illuminated the mountain path in front of them, but there was nothing to see but darkness.

"Let's hurry up and find this flower," John said.

Billy took his position beside John as the group continued following the tracks through the cave. The only sounds were footsteps and distant, trickling water.

"Whoa!" Billy pulled John backward to the cold cave floor. His flashlight shown ahead, where the track draped over the edge of a cliff. "Looks like the track collapsed right here."

All six flashlights aimed across the abyss. The gap was at least fifty yards. On the other side, the tracks picked up again after a sixty-foot drop in elevation.

"How do we get across that?" Shane wondered out loud.

"We can't," Billy whispered. He shone his flashlight on the moving water below, then quickly cut off his flashlight. "We need to go," he said. "Now."

"What?" John asked. "Why, dude?"

"Please," Billy said. "We need to go—there are tons of strigoi down there."

"Ah, don't worry about that," Shane said. "They're all asleep, right?" He nudged Billy to the side and pointed his flashlight down toward the flowing water. Hundreds of yellow eyes looked back at them. "RUN!"

The group bolted toward the entrance, their lights bouncing left, right, up, and down with every stride.

"Hurry," John shouted. "They're coming!"

The awakened strigoi screeched in anger. Their cry reverberated off every crevasse of the cave.

The group raced through the darkness, winding through the cave tunnels and nearly crying when they spotted the sunlight beaming in from the entrance ahead. Rachel and Cassie stepped out of the cave and into the light outside.

"Come on!" Rachel shouted back into the cave.

Shane and Billy rushed out of the cave, breathless.

"John! Cassie screamed. "Jimmy!"

Two small dots of light bounced toward the cave exit.

"I'm not gonna make it!" Jimmy yelled, three strides behind John.

"Yes, you are!" John insisted. "Run!"

Jimmy struggled to breathe as the sounds of flapping wings and screeching strigoi filled him with dread. Footsteps from the sunlit exit, Jimmy slipped on a damp rock and fell hard. His knee started bleeding immediately. The sound of wings grew louder.

"Get up, Jimmy!" John stood in the sunlight and screamed into the mountain.

Jimmy clawed his way back onto his feet, took two steps, and stumbled onto all fours. He could practically feel the wings of the strigoi as he crawled forward and dove face down into the sunlight.

The group cheered as Jimmy tried to catch his breath and gave a thumbs up.

"Jimmy," Cassie shouted, pointing at Jimmy's foot,

which was still covered in darkness, "your foot!"

Before she got the sentence out of her mouth, Jimmy was yanked back into the shadows.

"Jimmy!" John dug into his bag and grabbed the flare gun. He fired a shot into the darkness, lighting up the cave a bright red. Strigoi screeched and crawled away, hiding in the shadows. John emptied his bag looking for another flare. But he didn't need another one.

Jimmy crawled out of the cave, filthy and battered.

"Are you bit?" Billy lifted Jimmy's shirt and pant leg, looking for bites.

"No, I'm good," Jimmy mumbled before falling to his knees and throwing up.

"Ewe!" Shane shielded his eyes.

After a few minutes, Jimmy wiped the vomit from his mouth. He started to straighten his clothes but realized it was a lost cause. "Sorry about the puke, guys. I ain't ran that hard since football tryouts in seventh grade."

John hugged Jimmy. "Thought you were a goner, dude."

# CHAPTER 8

# THE CORN MAZE

Well, plan B didn't work. Neither did plan B, parts two or three. And we can't go back through the iron bridge entrance. Too risky. They'll be waiting for us.

It was Thursday, and the crew still hadn't found the second cave entrance. There were only three more days of fall break and nine days until John turned. The thought sent shivers down John's spine as he wrote in his journal, chronicling his symptomatic progression.

I'm super drowsy during the day, but with enough coffee I can push through usually. My fangs are permanently out and on display; however, I don't crave blood, and Mom and Dad didn't ask questions when Billy told them we were probably going to spend the whole break at The Roost.

The plan for the day was to take The Fury to the outskirts of Willow Springs. A road there sat between two huge cornfields, the only area left to search for mountain-cave access. Jimmy and Billy figured the tracks had to be hidden in the corn. John agreed. It would explain why they hadn't seen the tracks so far. They were hidden under cornstalks that were close to ten feet high.

This time around, no girls were invited.



The girls were upset at first, but the boys blamed it on The Fury's limited capacity.

"You good, man?" Billy called up the loft to John, who got dressed slowly for the day's mission.

"I'm alright," he said. "Just got a lot going on upstairs." He pointed at his head, but Billy didn't see him.

"Let's talk, dude." Billy climbed the loft ladder. "It's ten in the morning, we have all day."

John pulled a black leather belt through the loops in his pants. "I'm just tired, man. Tired of putting everyone in danger, tired of acting okay, tired of hiding things and keeping secrets."

"You can be real with me, man. I know you must be

scared. Shoot, I am. But dude, everyone loves you. They aren't risking their lives because they feel like they have to," Billy said. "They're doing it because they care about you."

"That's the worst part, man." John's voice broke, and he fought off tears. "They love me and are risking their lives for me, and I can't even tell them the truth."

"What do you mean? We all know the truth. That's why we're helping."

John reached into the desk drawer behind him and pulled out the file regarding Cassie's dad. "The day we stole the map from Jimmy's dad, I found this in his office." He tossed the folder to Billy. "It tells the real way Cassie's dad died, but I can't tell her. Jimmy begged me not to. His mom's sick with cancer and they need the money for her meds. If this gets out, Jimmy's dad could lose his job." John held his head in his hands. "But Cassie deserves to know."

Billy flipped through the file, then wrapped his arms around John. Pain oozed out of John's eyes in the form of tears. His body collapsed in Billy's embrace.

"It's going to be okay," Billy said.

John let out his fears and frustrations and heartache in a long, loud cry. Then he sucked back the snot and wiped away the tears. "I'll figure out that situation," he said through his teeth, "and I'll find a way to tell Cassie the truth without hurting Jimmy. But that isn't the worst part."

Billy backed out of the hug and kept his hands on John's shoulders. "What's the worst part then?"

"The thing that's been eating me up the most is what

the medicine man told me." John heard Billy's heart skip a beat. "You asked if there was a way to fully cure me from this, whatever it is. There is, according to the medicine man."

Billy sat quietly, patiently, eagerly for the answer.

"The only way to break the curse," John said, "is to find and kill the Shahidi."

"The Sha–what?" Billy asked. "Kill the what?"

"The Shahidi," John said. "It's what Native Americans call a witch. Well, a very specific witch."

Billy waited as John gathered his thoughts.

"The medicine man claimed the strigoi are like vampires in many ways, but not all," John continued. "To break the curse of a vampire, you kill the head vampire. But if you want to break the curse of a stryx, you have to kill the witch that holds the curse over them."

Billy considered this new, terrifying data for a moment. "Well, that's scary for sure," he admitted, "but the main objective right now is to find the Malus flower. That'll ease your symptoms, then we go from there."

"Should we tell the group?"

"Not yet, no."

"I just feel bad for hiding things and risking their lives," John cried, "without them even knowing the full truth."

"We aren't risking their lives." Billy gave a half-grin. "You and me are the only ones that are going in the mountain from here on out. And we will tell them everything—when the time is right."

"What about you?" John pressed. "What about your life?"

           Brock Enloe

"You're my little brother. Shoot," Billy said, "you're my only brother. I'd risk my life for you under any and every circumstance."

***

The thirty-minute drive to Willow Springs was accented with autumn-tinged mountain foliage. Reds, yellows, and oranges filled the horizon as The Fury sped toward their last hope of getting inside the mountain and finding the curative flower. Concrete turned to gravel and then dirt. After a few bumpy miles, Billy took a hard right, crashing The Fury through a line of cornstalks.

"Alright boys," he said, popping the driver's door open, "we're here."

"What if someone sees us?" Jimmy looked through The Fury's rear window and only saw cornstalks.

"Dude, no one's going to see us." John stepped out of the car and looked around. "I can't even see the road. Besides, I haven't seen a car in the last twenty minutes. There's nobody out here."

Jimmy and Shane pushed the front seat of The Fury forward, so they could get out.

"Whoa there, cowboys!" Billy shoved the driver's seat back into place. "John and I discussed this already. You fellas are staying here. We're hiking up to the mountain, just the two of us."

Shane slammed his hands against the back of the passenger seat. Jimmy looked confused.

"We have no clue what lies ahead or where to go," Billy said. "We just feel it's safer if the two of us go alone."

"No way!" Shane argued. "We rode this far, and we know what we're getting into. We're going with you guys."

"Trust me, it's better this way," John insisted. "Two here, two there. We go up and you guys stand guard at The Fury."

"Ugh!" Shane rolled his eyes. "So, I'm stuck here, where nothing's gonna happen? What if you need help?"

"Funny you should ask." Billy dropped a walkie-talkie onto the backseat. "We'll radio when we're back in the cornfield. Once we do, honk the horn, so we can find The Fury. Got it?"

"Yes." Jimmy snatched up the radio and smiled. "We got it."

Twenty minutes later, Shane stood on The Fury's hood, trying to track John and Billy, but it was all guesswork. John and Billy were way out of eyesight, hunting for the train track that led to the mouth of the cave. Shane grumbled at his rotten luck.

Jimmy leaned back on The Fury's hood and propped himself up on his elbows. "Dude, why are you pissed?"

"Because we should be out there. Aren't you mad?"

"Mad? Because I don't get to walk through a scary cornfield, hike miles up a mountain, and get chased by a blood sucking bat the size of a giant human?" Jimmy lay on his back with the walkie on his chest and his eyes closed. "Nope, I'm content right here."

Shane jumped off the hood and kicked at the nearest cornstalk as John's voice called through the walkie-talkie. They found the tracks and were following them up the mountain.

"They found the tracks!" Shane exclaimed.

Jimmy yawned. "Yep, I heard."

"Be safe and keep us updated," Shane said into the walkie, then looked at his watch. It was already one in the afternoon. Three more hours until dark.

***

Jimmy squirmed in The Fury's passenger seat. "Dude, they've been radio silent for too long. We need to call them on the walkie."

"You heard them," Shane said. "They directly told us not to radio them until they reached out to us."

"Yeah, I heard that—two and a half hours ago!" Jimmy rubbed his thumb along the ridge of the walkie's talk button. "We have thirty minutes until dark, then what?"

"I know, I know. Let's give them five more minutes. Call 'em too early, and those things might hear it. Not worth the risk."

Jimmy set the walkie-talkie on the dashboard and hung his right arm out the open window. As the darkness moved in, Jimmy pulled his arm back in the car and rolled his window halfway up.

"Yo Jimmy, you ever see that scary movie, *Children of the Corn*?"

"Shut up, man."

"What's wrong? I thought you liked sitting in the car in the middle of a giant cornfield in the middle of nowhere with blood-sucking bat things flapping around nearby."

"Dude, I mean it," Jimmy said sternly. "Shut up!"

Shane held his hands up defensively. "Sorry, bro. I, uh, I joke when I'm nervous."

Jimmy huffed. "It's been long enough." He snatched the walkie-talkie from the dashboard and handed it to Shane. "Radio them."

Shane held the walkie and took a deep breath. "Come in, come in. Are you guys okay?"

The walkie returned to gentle static.

"Keep trying them," Jimmy insisted.

"Hello, are you guys there?"

Nothing. Time crawled past, as the descending darkness was completely settled in around The Fury. Shane and Jimmy sat quietly in the seats, rocking back and forth.

Wind swept through the field, causing the cornstalks to sway and brush against each other and sing out in an eerie chorus. Shane rocked in his chair, biting his nails. Then, a new sound.

"Mayday, Mayday!" John's voice screamed through the walkie.

Shane reached for the walkie, dropped it in the floorboard, picked it up, and slammed down the talk button. "John, what's going on?"

"Honk!" John yelled. "Honk the horn!"

Jimmy reached over Shane's lap and slammed the palm of his hand against the middle of the steering wheel. An annoying, unnatural honk rang out.

Shane covered one ear and shouted through the walkie, "What's going on? Come on guys, talk to us!"

"It's right on top of us" John screamed back, his voice muffled by a stryx screech.

"Did you hear that?" Shane turned to Jimmy, wide-eyed. "The screech of that thing came through the walkie!"

"That wasn't from the walkie!" Jimmy pointed at the giant winged creature soaring above the corn toward them and hurried into the backseat.

Shane laid on the horn, but the stryx kept its eyes on the ground, scanning the field for its prey. "If that thing is above you right now," Shane shouted into the walkie, "run straight for about fifty yards and you'll run into The Fury."

Shane started The Fury and turned on the bright lights, hit the horn one more time, then crawled into the backseat, his eyes focused on the stryx as it dove into the corn.

Somewhere among the cornstalks, John and Billy dashed toward the sound of the horn.

"Come on!" Billy shouted.

Bobbing and weaving, they saw The Fury's lights just before the stryx swooped down and knocked John to the ground. John rolled to a hard stop and looked up at the beast.

"Help!"

The creature stood over John and let out a horrific screech and flashed his long, blood-stained fangs. It lunged at John, and then it was gone.

When John sat up, he saw Billy wrestling with the beast. As the sparring pair rolled over stalks of corn, John shuffled through his bag, found what he needed, and leapt to his feet. He could hear the fight, but it was too dark to see.

John stomped through the corn. "Billy!"

Billy screamed. John took two hard steps to the right and there they were, Billy and the stryx, fighting to the death. John reared back with both hands and drove the stake through the creature's back. The stryx let out an ear-ringing shriek, and dark, thick blood spewed onto Billy's white shirt. Billy pushed the beast off of him and grabbed John's extended hand.

"You, okay?" John asked. "You bit?"

"I'm good. Let's go."

Inside The Fury, Shane and Jimmy kept their eyes glued to the windows.

Shane raised a finger. "I think I hear something."

Jimmy scooted to the middle of the back seat and held his breath. He exhaled quietly, then whispered, "I don't hear any—"

A bloody hand slammed against the window in front of Shane's face.

"Let us in!"

Shane and Jimmy screamed.

"Let us in!" John pressed his face against the window.

Jimmy and Shane screamed again.

"Come on," Billy cried from the other side, "unlock the door!"

Still trembling, Shane and Jimmy unlocked the front doors. Billy and John stumbled in, and Billy immediately slammed the car into drive.

"What happened?" Jimmy blurted out.

"We killed one," John said.

"You what?" Jimmy asked.

"We killed a stryx." Billy looked into the rearview mirror suspiciously.

		Brock Enloe

"Billy," John shouted, "look out!"

Billy swore under his breath and swerved sharply to avoid a stryx standing in the middle of the road. The Fury slid left and flipped three times, landing on its side in a pile of dust and broken cornstalks. The four of them scrambled out of the car.

"Help me flip this thing!" John shouted.

After a three count, they heaved The Fury back on its wheels. A stryx screeched nearby, sending all four boys back into the car, with John in the driver's seat.

"Go!" Billy said. "Drive!"

As The Fury raced through the night, the sound of screeching stryx faded. Eventually, the night calmed, and John listened with interest to his friends' heartbeats slowing to normal. He eased off the gas pedal, bringing The Fury to a leisurely pace, as the walkie-talkies sounded.

"Hello, anyone there? John, Billy, anyone?"

It was Cassie. Just hearing her voice got John's heart pumping fast. He grabbed the walkie-talkie and told Cassie she was coming in loud and clear, and they were just getting back to Burdine. Cassie suggested everyone crash at her house. Rachel was staying with her, and Cassie's mom was working and wouldn't be home until lunch the next day.

With no objection from the other guys, John accepted the offer. It would be nice to spend a night away from The Roost.

A few minutes later, John pulled The Fury up at Cassie's house. Smoke seeped out from under the hood, and the engine puttered to a stop.

Cassie and Rachel gasped as the boys fell through the

front door, banged up and bleeding.

"Babe!" Rachel rushed to Billy and hugged him. "Are you guys okay?"

John rubbed his neck, staring into the distance, as Cassie brushed back his curly hair and wiped blood from his head.

After showers, the whole crew sat in Cassie's living room. The hot water wore off some of the evening's shock. Shane pointed at Jimmy, and everyone started laughing.

Jimmy settled into an oversized armchair. "What's so funny?"

"I don't know," Shane said, "maybe the fact that you're posted up on Cassie's dad's favorite chair, eating a slice of pizza, with your body squeezed tightly inside Cassie's pink Def Leppard T-shirt."

Jimmy sighed and took another bite of pizza.

"So, tell us what happened tonight." Cassie nestled against John. "Did you find the flower?"

Shane and Rachel leaned forward, and Jimmy stopped chewing, eager to hear John's response.

"Short answer," John started, "no, we didn't find the flower."

Billy grunted, then put his arm around Rachel and leaned back.

"It took me and Billy about forty minutes to hike to the entrance, where the tracks just stopped. I don't know if they were buried or what, but we couldn't see them anymore. So, we wandered into the mountain and searched around for hours, until we got lost."

Billy coughed. The crew turned to him for his input. Billy underhand waved at John to continue.

          Brock Enloe

"Well," John said, "after an hour or so, we found the exit, and it was already dusk. So, we rushed down the mountain, trying to stay hidden from the strigoi that were nearby."

"And we did a pretty good job of it, too," Billy said, "until Shane radioed us on the walkie."

Shane glared at Jimmy. "Told you we shouldn't have called them."

Jimmy sank deeper into the chair, as if trying to hide.

"Once they sounded the walkie, the strigoi heard us." John rubbed his fangs against his lower lip. "We sprinted to the corn for cover, but one stryx was stalking us. That's why John radioed for Shane and Jimmy to honk—to locate The Fury and get the stryx off our back."

"That's messed up," Jimmy mumbled.

"Well, the distraction didn't work," Billy said, "so chill out."

John opened a can of grape soda. "You know we're just kidding. We needed to find The Fury." He continued to tell the story, including the part about Billy rescuing him from the stryx and how he returned the favor by plunging a stake into the stryx's heart.

Jimmy and Shane hung on every word. Cassie and Rachel were simultaneously grossed out and enamored with their boyfriends' bravery.

"I can't believe you guys actually killed a stryx!" Shane said. "And without me!"

"So, you killed a stryx and then drove away." Rachel bit her lip. "Then what happened to The Fury?"

"Uh, I flipped it," Billy said. "There was another stryx in the road, and I swerved to miss it."

The group busted out laughing again. "Well," Cassie said, "I'm just glad you guys are all okay."

"Yeah, it's good that we're all okay, but..."

"But what, Shane?" Rachel asked.

Shane set his pizza on a white paper plate. "How are we going to get the flower now?"

All eyes turned to John. He took a long, slow draw from his grape soda, then set the can down. He wiped his face with a paper napkin. "Y'all aren't gonna like the plan, but it's our only hope."

"And what would that be?" Shane questioned. "What is our only hope?"

"We go through the entrance at the iron bridge."

"Already tried that," Shane said.

"The tracks collapsed," Jimmy said. "There's no way we can get across the abyss."

"I know," John said. "That's why we're gonna repel down into it."

             Brock Enloe

# CHAPTER 9

# THE DESCENT

John held a finger on the map. "If we tie the rope to a rock here, it should stretch to the bottom of the ravine."

"How do we know that a rock we find in the dark won't break loose?" Billy patted his legs. "I say we tie it off to the handcar."

"But the handcar won't hold our weight," John said.

"An empty handcar won't," Billy said, "but if there are people on it..."

John ran his tongue under his protruding fangs, one at a time. "We agreed that you and me are the only ones risking our lives from here on out."

"And we will be," Billy said, matter-of-factly. "You and me will be the only ones repelling down to certain death. The others will just be sitting on the handcar, hanging out."

Shane walked across The Roost. "Better than getting left out again. Right, Jimmy?"

Jimmy sat up on the couch. "What's that?"

"Nothing, Jimmy." Billy ran his hands along the edges of the coffee table. "John and I are trying to find a way to anchor the rope down without having you guys tag along."

"What?" Cassie cried. "No way! You guys aren't going in alone."

"We can't put you guys in danger," John said. "Not any more than we already have."

"That's not your call." Jimmy cleared his throat and pushed his chest out. "It's up to us."

Rachel looked at Jimmy with newfound respect. "He's right, and we're going to help."

John exhaled slowly. "Let's go through the plan."

It was complete insanity. The group would ride the handcar to the boarded-up entrance, then push it to the pit. Next, Billy or John would tie a rope to the front of the handcar, repel into the abyss, swing to the other side, retrieve the mythical Malus flower, and get out of there as fast as possible. They were going to do it at night, when the strigoi were less likely to be in the cave.

"That's it?" Jimmy looked from John to Billy, then back again. His previous confidence had left. "That's the plan?"

"Simple," Billy said, "yet effective."

Cassie grabbed John's hand and looked into his eyes. "You think this will work?"

"It has to," John said, bowing his head. It's the only option left on the table."

A few hours later, a pile of flares lay on top of what John deemed "the longest rope in Burdine." Shane pulled

     Brock Enloe

burgers off the grill, which the group ate immediately. A tinge of hope, a hint of normalcy filtered through The Roost and left Billy sentimental for simpler times, for nights listening to Cardinals games at The Roost.

"We'll have plenty more of those nights," John insisted. "We just gotta find the flower and get this over with."

"I hope man," Shane said. "In every movie with two brothers, both never make it to the end."

Jimmy punched Shane's arm, hard. "This is not the time!"

"I'm just saying," Shane said, flipping a burger.

"Name three movies where the brothers die," Billy said.

"*Red Dawn*," Shane started. "The older brother gets killed at the end."

"Okay, that's one." Billy raised a finger. "Two more."

"*Top Gun*."

"Are you serious?" John asked.

"What?" Shane placed a burger on Cassie's plate. "The dude broke his neck and died."

"Oh, man." Billy rubbed his forehead. "That wasn't his brother, you idiot."

"Are you sure it wasn't his brother?" Shane asked.

"Proof positive that Shane doesn't know what he's talking about," John said. "We'll be fine. In and out, easy-peasy." A wide grin spread across John's face, but fear peeked out from underneath.

"So, can we see the handcar now?" Rachel looked past the group at the covered handcar. "Y'all have had it hidden since we got back."

Jimmy let out a giant burp, which got a hearty congratulations from Shane. Then the pair walked to the handcar and grabbed the sheet.

"Now, before we unveil this, you should know something." Shane lowered his voice. "This thing has been enhanced for speed, built for durability, and is ranked number one in the stryx safety index, as it is coated in garlic paint. It features handcrafted wooden stake armor guaranteed to protect the passengers inside, all while providing a smooth, pleasant ride along Burdine's long-abandoned tracks. This beauty has—"

"Shut up!" Billy joked. "Show us the thing already."

Shane paused to gather his thoughts. "As I was saying, before I was rudely interrupted, this beauty has been equipped with the most efficient stryx-killing weapons of our time. Truly state-of-the-art, complete with built-in holy-water guns—four of them, to be exact. Two on the front, two on the back. No stryx will dare to get close to this thing."

Rachel and Cassie chuckled at Shane's antics. The boys groaned.

"Without further ado," Shane announced, "I present to you the Tactical Overnight Adaptable Stryx Tank, TOAST for short."

Shane and Jimmy yanked on the sheet to unveil the updated handcar. The once-open cart was now encased in a rusty, sheet-metal body that glistened with garlic powder. Rows of wooden stakes stuck out at every angle, held in place by twine and duct tape.

"I'm dying!" Billy wheezed and doubled over. "It hurts to laugh. TOAST?"

"The only thing that's gonna be toast is us!" John belted out.

Jimmy stomped on the ground. "Come on, guys. We worked hard on this thing."

"Doesn't look like it," Cassie said under her breath.

"Okay, it's not the nicest ride," Jimmy admitted. "But check this out." He grabbed a yellow string sticking out of the top of the roof and pulled.

John tilted his head and grinned. "Whoa! The door opens from the top. Okay, that's cool."

"It's like the DeLorean!" Jimmy said. "You know, from *Back to the Future*."

Shane stepped in front of the updated handcar. "My favorite part is the front window. We needed a way to see out that wouldn't let the strigoi in, so—"

He pointed at the window, made with a cross in the center.

"Smart idea!" John patted Shane on the back. "Still looks like a spiky turtle though."

"More like a porcupine," Billy chimed in.

"Looks can be deceiving." Shane banged a hand against the exterior. "But remember—this thing is going to save our lives."

The Roost darkened. Night fell outside. It was time to head for the mountain. The laughter died away. The group loaded their supplies in the handcar, took their seats inside, and latched the door shut. John released the brake, and he and Billy pedaled into the darkness. Jimmy and Shane peered out, looking for signs of strigoi. Rachel and Cassie checked the supplies and split them into two book bags—one for John, one for Billy. After a tense ride through the dark, the handcar's headlight stared down the entrance of the cave.

"Everyone stay alert," John said. "We're going in."

Cassie handed John his bag and gave him a quick kiss. "I love you," she said.

Rachel does the same for Billy, but the kiss was much, much longer.

The brothers slung their backpacks over their shoulders and exited the handcar. Rachel and Cassie shifted to the pedal seats and released the brake. John and Billy pushed the handcar through the entrance and toward the unknown. A slight decline made the pushing easy. In only a few minutes, they reached their destination. Cassie engaged the brake as John secured the rope to the handcar.

Rachel whispered through the handcar's rickety exterior, "Remember your promise, Billy Daggon."

"I will," he promised. "I'll be right back."

While John and Jimmy checked the walkie-talkies at the lowest possible volume, Billy crawled to the edge of the pit and shown his light down. He turned and gave John a thumbs-up. "No bat eyes in view," he whispered, his rapid heartbeat pounding in John's ears.

"Relax," John mouthed.

"What if that thing's down there?" Billy asked.

"The Shahidi?"

Billy pushed away from the ledge and stood up. "That name gives me the creeps. Just call it the witch. Is it down there?"

"Let's hope not."

"In and out," Billy muttered.

               Brock Enloe

John tossed the rope over the edge and began to descend, guided by Billy's flashlight. The handcar rocked gently at the weight.

Rachel turned her head and covered her eyes. "I can't watch," she whimpered, as Billy began his descent.

A few moments later, the handcar shook violently, and the handbrake squealed.

"We made the jump across," John reported through the walkie. "We're on the other side."

"Roger that," Jimmy replied. "Going quiet now. Check in every fifteen minutes to let us know you're okay."

"Ten-four."

John pulled the rope as far as it would go, then laid it down quietly. He and Billy followed the tracks around one bend after another, the air growing heavier and colder and wetter with each step.

"How far to the center of the cave?" Billy said. "What's the map show?"

John stood in a puddle and pulled the map out of his bag. It showed a steep turn, a drop-off, and then a big, open room. Billy nodded and pointed at his watch. "It's been almost fifteen minutes."

John places the map in his bag and grabs the walkie. "Performing check-in number one. You guys okay? What's your status?"

The static only lasted for a moment before Jimmy's voice broke through. "All good up here. What about you guys?"

"So far, so good." John took a breath. "Approaching the heart of the mountain. We'll be in touch shortly."

John and Billy shuffled around a sharp turn, just as the map showed. Soon as the path straightened out again, the tracks declined in elevation until they became completely submerged underwater.

Billy's flashlight reflected off the water. "What now?"

John pointed his light at a small opening above the water. "The big room has to be on the other side of this pool of water. If it is, the flower's got to be in there, too."

"It's like twenty yards to the opening though."

John tossed his backpack on a pile of rocks nearby. "Guess we're swimming." He tossed his shirt on top of his backpack.

"Shoot, shoot, shoot!" Billy stripped off his shirt and laid it and his pack beside John's pile.

"Don't forget the container," John said, stepping into the water. "For the flower."

"Wait on me, man!" Billy whisper-shouted. He raffled through his bag, grabbed the container, and rushed to the water's edge.

"Bro!" Billy pulled his foot out of the water. His body shivered, and his teeth chattered.

John exhaled like a yoga guru and tried to ignore the sound of Billy's racing heart. "It's not too bad."

"Of course it's not cold for you." Billy stepped back into the water and grinned in the dark. "Dracula."

"I'm not a vampire, and I have no intentions of becoming one." John waded farther in the water, forcing Billy to speed up or be left behind. "That's why we are down here wading through this icy water."

Chest deep in the murky cold water, the boys inched along toward the opening in the distance. Droplets of

     Brock Enloe

water fell from the cave ceiling, some plopping into the water, others splashing against the boys' bare shoulders.

John's breathing sped up. The water was cold, even for someone in the process of becoming a cold-blooded stryx. When they reached the opening, the frigid water reached the top of their shoulders.

"Follow me." John lowered himself deeper in the water and slid underneath the small opening. Once through to the other side, he grabbed Billy's hands and pulled him through the crack. Billy spit out a mouthful of water and got to his feet, then the pair took in their surroundings.

They were inside the large cave room. The massive underground lake covered most of the area, except for a small rock island in the middle. A set of train tracks rose out of the water, ran the length of the rock island, and continued through a tunnel on the far side of the lake.

"W-w-well," Billy said, "not much to see here."

"Wait!" John held his light on the rock island. There, in the middle of the small protruding rock was something that looked very un-rocklike. It looked delicate, alive.

"No w-way!"

"Way," John whispered. "There it is, the Malus flower."

The boys turned to each other for a quick air high-five. A short swim and an even shorter climb were all that stood between them and the flower.

"Alright," John said with a shrug, "you stay here and work the light."

Billy rubbed his arms for warmth. "How d-d-deep do you think the water is out th-there?" Billy questions, with his teeth still chattering from the frigid water.

John dropped into the dark water and disappeared. He popped his head above the surface and wiped water from his face. "Real deep. Can't walk. Gotta swim."

The water temperature continued to drop as John got farther from Billy and closer to the island. John kicked hard, but his tennis shoes and jeans didn't let him swim too quickly. By the time he pulled himself onto the island, he was panting, and his skin prickled with cold chills.

One cautious foothold at a time, John ascended the island wall, slipping on the slick limestone, but never losing his grip altogether. Soon, the Malus flower was in reach. John pulled himself onto the island's crest and fumbled the container out of his pocket with shaky hands. He plucked several flowers and laid them inside before sealing the container.

He raised the container, so Billy could see. Billy focused his flashlight on John's hands, just as a whooshing sound came from the pitch black behind him.

"Jump!" Billy yelled.

A stryx dove at John and pierced his shoulder in a swift, powerful swoop. John tumbled off the rock and splashed into the cold water below. He emerged coughing and gasping for air, clinging to the container and swimming toward Billy's light, leaving a thin pink blood trail in his wake.

"Come on!" Billy yelled.

John kicked and kicked, until Billy grabbed his hand. Billy yanked John out of the lake and back through the low, watery underpass.

"You get the flower?"

          Brock Enloe

"Yeah, I got the flower." John walked beside Billy in chest-deep water, desperate to get on dry land. "I also got a stryx talon and lost my flashlight."

"Dude!" Billy eyed the sharp claw lodged in John's left shoulder. "You okay?"

"I'll be fine," John insisted. "Let's just get out of here."

The two stepped out of the water and scurried to their abandoned backpacks and shirts. John handed Billy the flower. Billy shoved it into his bag while John radioed the others.

"About time you guys called!" Jimmy was on the other end. "Are y'all okay?"

"We ran into some company," John said.

John pulled his shirt over his head, then winced. The talon caught on the sleeve. Pain shot through John's body. He clenched his fists, then balled up the shirt and tossed it on the ground. Billy pulled his shirt on and strapped his backpack on tight as his flashlight faded.

"Are you guys okay?" Jimmy repeated.

"We got the flower," John said.

Billy used his dying flashlight to scan his bag's contents. He grabbed three flares.

"Now you boys get back to us," Rachel said through the walkie. "Come on, Billy!"

"You heard her." John slung his bag over his right shoulder. "Come on, Billy."

Bright red flare light illuminated the path in seven-minute increments. In less than fifteen minutes, the boys were down to their last flare. If the rest of their exit took more than seven minutes, they would be as good as blind. John unscrewed the lid and held the striker against the top, as a strange, shrill cackle echoed behind them.

"Did you hear that?" Billy screamed. "Light the flare! Light the flare!"

John struck the flare against the damp cave wall, sending a burst of red down the tunnel.

"Run!" John shoved Billy down the path and started to sprint.

Behind them, a lanky human-like creature gave chase, its stringy hair bouncing on its head, its claws spread out widely, nearly scraping the sides of the tunnel. John pointed the flare backward and shouted again: "Run!" This time, his voice sounded unfamiliar, almost nonhuman. It was loud and powerful, as if strong enough to shake the walls of the cave. Then, it did.

Something cracked behind Billy. He turned as the ceiling collapsed, blocking the tunnel just before they reached the gaping crevasse. The chasing creature hissed through the cracks and clawed at the rubble.

"It's trapped in there for now, but hurry!" John said. "Go, go, go!"

Billy grabbed the rope and swung across the gap. The handcar rattled and shook as he climbed to the top. Shane helped him up, then cheered John on.

John sandwiched the flare between his shoulder and backpack strap, then tightened the strap before swinging across the abyss. On the other side, he slammed against the rock wall, pushing the talon deeper into his shoulder. He let out a cry and squeezed the rope.

"Come on!" Billy yelled. "Climb!"

John grunted, then pulled himself up slowly, hand over hand. An arm's length from the top, he tossed the

          Brock Enloe

flare up to Billy and reached for Shane's outstretched arm. Then, the rope went slack.

In an instant, John was swallowed up by the darkness. Shane grabbed the rope and struggled to hold fast, but the rope was slipping through his fingers.

"Help!" he yelled.

Jimmy pulled on the rope, while Billy tied a knot in the end. "Bring it over here," Billy said. The three of them moved the rope to the right side of the cave and wedged the knotted end between two boulders. Billy grabbed the fizzling flare off the ground. "Pull him up!"

Cassie turned on the handcar's light, just as something popped over the edge. It was John's head. The handcar light reflected in his eyes, which went from tired relief to terrified surprise.

"Cassie," John shouted. "Behind you!"

Cassie and Rachel ducked as a group of screeching strigoi flew over the handcar toward John. Billy ran toward the edge, pleading with John to climb faster, and then he was airborne. His feet kicked helplessly in the air, as a seething stryx dropped him past John and into the abyss.

John and Shane screamed as Billy plummeted past them. A cluster of strigoi plunged into the darkness and surrounded Billy's falling body, their wings spread wide and smothered the flare's final efforts at light.

"Billy!" Tears gushed from John's eyes and dripped off his face, falling toward his brother's blood-gurgling cries.

# CHAPTER 10

# THE DEATH KNELL

Jimmy bailed out of the handcar and slammed The Roost's double doors shut. The others climbed out slowly, their faces stained with tears. Rachel sobbed uncontrollably and let Cassie help her out of the TOAST. Feeling a need to do something, Shane unloaded the supplies. John slumped on the ground, shirtless and covered in mud and blood, leaning against the wall and staring off into space.

"He didn't even want to go in there," Rachel cried. "He told me earlier today he was so scared, but he had no choice, that it was his little brother and, and, and..."

John's lip quivered. He buried his head in his hands, then his shoulders shook—slowly at first, and then violently. "Why?" John tore at his hair and rocked. "Why!"

"I'm sorry, but we shouldn't wait." Jimmy offered John a folded towel. "You may want to bite on this."

John grabbed the towel and set it in his lap.

"Shane, can you hold him in place?" Jimmy put one hand on John's back and wrapped the other around the talon. "John, I'm sorry, but this is going to hurt."

With no countdown or buildup, Jimmy pulled on the stryx talon. John's skin raised at the effort, but John showed no emotion. After a brief struggle, the discolored talon came loose. Jimmy tossed it to the ground, then took the towel out of John's lap and pressed it against the wound.

"Here, hold this on," he said to Shane. "I need to go wash my hands."

Shane held the towel firmly against John's shoulder, impressed by John's stoicism. "I know things are bleak," Shane said, "but we got the flower."

"No, we didn't," John's growled.

Shane looked at the others with confusion. The others stared at John.

"We didn't get it." John grabbed the towel out of Shane's hands and worked his way to his feet with no hands. "It was in Billy's bag."

With that, John held out his arms and collapsed to the ground.

Cassie scrambled to his side. "It's going to be okay, John. Just wait, you'll—"

"Nothing is okay!" John crawled to the coffee table and flipped it over, sending empty pizza boxes, used paper plates, and a handful of dishes across the floor of The Roost.

"John!" Cassie shouted. "John, stop—look at me!"

John flung his flashlight against the wall, shattering

the plastic casing. Two D-size batteries tumbled to the ground and rolled to a stop. John fell to his back and pounded the ground with his fists.

"John, look at me," Cassie begged, rubbing the side of his face.

"My brother is..."

Cassie draped an arm over John as he wept. "Shhh..." When she lifted her hand, it was smeared in red. She waved at Jimmy, who grabbed the discarded towel, sat cross-legged beside John, and held the towel on John's shoulder.

Cassie thanked him, kissed John's shoulder, and climbed the loft ladder. She flung the desk drawers open and rummaged through them for bandages. As she did, something else caught her eye: a manila folder with her dad's name on it. She hesitated, then opened the file. She read one page, then another. Tears bubbled and fell from her eyes.

She climbed down the ladder and stomped toward John.

Jimmy looked up. "Find any bandages?"

Cassie tossed the file in John's lap. "Did you know?"

John answered with a simple nod.

"You weren't going to tell me?"

"I wanted to," John started, "but..."

"But what?" Cassie snatched the folder.

"But..." John threw his hands in the air. "But, I don't know."

"I can't believe you." Cassie spun on her heels and marched to the loft ladder. Halfway up, she turned and glared at John. "I'm glad you're alive, but we are over."

Hours pass as the crew awaited the safety of sunrise. The only sounds were sighs and whispers from Cassie and Rachel in the loft. The longer the silence rolled on, the louder John's thoughts and others' heartbeats became.

"I have to go back." John's eyes danced from one friend to another.

"Are you crazy?" Jimmy exclaimed.

"My brother's still in there. I have to go back."

"John," Jimmy said softly. "He's dead. Billy's dead."

"We don't know that!" John shouted.

"John, we saw him die." Jimmy looked at Shane for support.

Rachel and Cassie watched on from the loft at first, then made their way quietly down the ladder.

John rose to his feet and shook his head. "No, we saw him fall. We did not see him die."

"If you go back in there," Shane said, "you'll never make it out."

John clenched his fists and licked the bottom of his fangs. "I'm dead anyway."

The front door opened, and then a streak of sunlight broke into The Roost. Rachel held the door open, as Cassie stepped toward the threshold.

"Cassie, wait!" John pleaded.

"I thought you cared about me," Cassie said through tears. "I loved you!"

"Loved?" John asked.

Cassie sniveled, then walked out of The Roost.

"Cassie!" John ran to the door but stopped short of chasing her. Instead, he watched her pass into the woods and out of sight.

Rachel squeezed past John awkwardly, before racing to catch up to Cassie. Then Jimmy bumped against John as he walked out of The Roost.

"You, too?" John asked.

"You totally screwed me, man—and my dad." Jimmy's eyes were heavy with sadness. "I'm out," he mumbled.

John plopped down on the couch and stared at the ceiling, looking for answers that weren't there.

"Don't worry about them, man. They'll come around," Shane insisted. "And we'll get that flower, promise. Billy would want that."

***

John slept fitfully in the loft, plagued by nightmares that all took place in the cave. When he jolted awake, he was drenched in sweat. He crawled out of bed and down from the loft. Stepping over the trash and broken dishes, his heart sunk. What had he done to his friends?

Outside, the sun began to set.

Inside, John was all alone. No Billy, no friends, and no Cassie. John craved human connection, so he threw a few things in his bag and headed home. He tucked his fangs inside his lips and pushed through the front door. But there was no warm welcome. Just an empty house and a small sticky note that read, *Your dad and I went out. Won't be back until late.*

John crumpled the note into a ball and stumbled to his bedroom. His lip quivered upon seeing his brother's side of the room. Through blurred vision, he barely made out Billy's basketball jersey hanging above his bed.

 Brock Enloe

After a long, hot shower, John lay on his bed, fully dressed. It was nighttime, and he was wide awake. The front door opened. It was his parents. John heard their footsteps and their heartbeats before their voices.

"Come on darling, let's go to bed," Mr. Daggon said. "We have church in the morning."

"Just give me a second," Mrs. Daggon replied. "I'm going to check on the boys."

Mrs. Daggon took a handful of hurried steps before Mr. Daggon called out to her. "You know they don't sleep here anymore. They're teenagers. Probably camping out at The Roost or staying at Jimmy's house."

She paused. "Oh, you're right."

"I'm always right," joked Mr. Daggon.

Their footsteps faded away, and John could barely hear their hearts through their closed bedroom door. John's watch read a few minutes past midnight. With no grand plan to carry out, he reached into his bag and grabbed his journal.

A million thoughts fought for his attention and came out in short, painful bursts.

> Nothing will ever be the same, and it's all my fault.
>
> My brother is dead, and it's my fault.
>
> I lost Cassie, too.
>
> And I hurt my best friend, Jimmy. Because I held onto a file.
>
> I have less than a week until I turn, and I can't give up. That would mean Billy died for nothing. But if Billy isn't dead...

"Rise and Shine!" Mrs. Daggon swung open the door to John's bedroom. "Get up and get ready for church!"

John sat on the desk chair, looking out the window.

"Your father thought you weren't here last night," Mrs. Daggon said, "but I saw your wadded-up towel in the bathroom.

"I'm not going."

"Excuse me, mister?" Mrs. Daggon fluttered around the room, looking for something to clean. The only thing there was John's backpack. "You know we don't miss church! And where's Billy?"

"He's not here." John squinted at the rising sun. "He's at, uh, Shane's, I think."

***

In the wooden church pew, John fought against the stuffy, warm environment and calming voice of the preacher to stay awake. He began fading when someone pinched his ear.

"Sit up!" his mother whispered sternly. "Your father and I did not let you stay in that barn just so you could sleep in church."

John apologized. He pressed his back against the pew and opened his eyes as wide as they would go.

Oblivious to the family drama unfolding in front of him, the bald-headed pastor licked his thumb and opened his Bible. "Turn to Matthew seven," he said. "We'll be reading verses thirteen and fourteen."

Eager to stay awake and avoid another pinch from his mom, John grabbed a pew Bible to follow along.

     Brock Enloe

"Enter by the narrow gate," the preacher continued. "For the gate is wide and the way is easy that leads to destruction, and those who enter by it are many. For the gate is narrow and the way is hard that leads to life, and those who find it are few."

The words swam in John's vision. He blinked twice to wash away the blurriness.

"These are Jesus's words." The pastor pressed his hands into the wooden pulpit. "Let's read it again."

John followed along again, bouncing his finger on the page in rhythm with the preacher's voice.

"For the gate is narrow!" The preacher stepped back from the microphone, as someone called out *Hallelujah!* from the back of the congregation. The pastor moved forward. "And the way is hard that leads to life."

Another pause, another *Hallelujah!* Then, something clicked inside John's head.

"That's it!" John leapt to his feet.

"John Mark Daggon!" Mr. Daggon's face burned red. "Sit down right this moment!"

John bent down and kissed his mother on the cheek. "There's another way in," he said. "I've got to go."

***


At The Roost, John grabbed the map stolen from Mr. Bardot's office and traced the path where The Narrows exited the cave. It weaved through the giant room with the Malus flower and the base of the pit into which Billy fell.

"Thank you, Jesus."

Fueled by mediocre coffee, John spent the day planning his mission, prepping his gear, and headbanging to Iron Maiden.

His bag full of hand flares, a flower container, and an extra flashlight, he strapped four wooden stakes to his pant leg, put on the cross necklace Cassie made for him, and tied a garlic-soaked bandanna across his forehead. He popped open the box of World War two items from Jimmy's grandpa and took out a black-handled bowie knife. "Just like Rambo," he said, attaching it to his hip. "And a parachute?" He strapped the old rig to his back. "Don't mind if I do."

Dressed and equipped, he sat down with pen and paper before walking into the setting sun for Operation 713: The Narrows.

# CHAPTER 11

# THE NARROWS

Shane stared at the note left on the coffee table inside The Roost. The paper fell to the floor as Shane rushed up the loft ladder to grab the walkie.

"Guys, come in!" he shouted into the walkie-talkie. "We have a problem!"

He released the talk button and waited. No one responded. He repeated his call several times, his voice rising in pitch with the repetition.

Finally, Jimmy's voice cut through the walkie. "What, dude? I'm trying to enjoy my last night before school starts back in the morning."

"He went to the mountain. Alone!"

"You gotta be clearer than that," Jimmy said. "Who went to the mountain?"

"Who do you think?" Shane yelled. "John!"

"Is he okay?" Jimmy's voice throbbed with fear. "Did he make it back?"

"I don't know," Shane said. "I came to The Roost to check on him and found a note. It said he found another way into the mountain, and I'm bugging out, man!"

Jimmy told Shane to stay calm and stay put. He would let Cassie know what happened and would be at The Roost in fifteen minutes.

"Be careful," Shane said, "it's almost dark."

***

With the last bit of daylight disappearing, Cassie and Rachel slid into The Roost and locked the door behind them. Cassie went straight for the note and pulled it out of Shane's hand.

"Hey." Shane chewed on his fingernails and spit a small piece on the floor. "Rachel, I didn't expect to see you."

Cassie eyed the letter, scanning it for reassurance or a reason to fear.

"Read it out loud," Rachel said.

Cassie's eyes reached the bottom of the page, then leapt back to the top.

> To the group, better yet to my family…
> I apologize for causing a rift between us all. I love each and every one of you, and you guys are all I have left. If I make it back, I will desperately do what I can to repair our relationships, but if I don't return, I want you guys to know that I am truly sorry for everything.
> I believe I've found another way into the mountain, and I have to go check. Billy would

          Brock Enloe

have wanted me to, and I can't let him die for nothing. By the time you guys read this, I will have ~~stolen~~ borrowed Shane's boat and gotten halfway across the lake. My plan is to enter the mountain using The Narrows. The entrance is in the small lagoon just before the dam, and it should put me fairly close to the flower.

If I don't make it back, Shane, you can find your boat parked in the back of the lagoon.

Once I tie the boat off, I'll swim under the cave wall and wade through the tunnels up and into the cavern room that holds the flower.

It's a difficult trek, but it's my only option. I can't give up...not now.

Again, I'm sorry for everything. I hope to see you guys in the morning. Shane, please make sure Cassie gets the special note I left for her.

I love you all.

—John

Cassie folded and unfolded the letter over and over. Shane handed Cassie an envelope with her name on it, the "special note" John mentioned.

Tension bounced off The Roost's walls and rafters. Everyone wanted to do something to help John, but they couldn't do it now. It was too dark. They'd have to wait until dawn or risk getting picked off by strigoi.

While they sat and stressed, John boated toward The Narrows. A lantern hung from the front of the boat, issuing a weak orb of light for navigation. Fog hugged the water surface, reducing visibility even further. John strained to see and guide the boat.

October winds sent waves crashing against the hull. A small crack in the fog showed a colony of strigoi circling the mountain peak. Chills ran down John's back and his heart raced as the strigoi's screeches cut through the fog.

He drifted through the lagoon, careful to move slowly and leave only a slight ripple in his wake. After steering the boat under the cave ceiling, he hopped out and tied the boat off to a stalagmite pillar hanging from the roof.

With his backpack strapped on both shoulders, John moved his hands underwater slowly. After a moment, he felt a slight movement underwater where The Narrows exited the mountain. He took a deep breath, then plummeted into the water and under the cave wall.

When he emerged on the other side, the humidity was stifling. John pulled his flashlight from his bag and began to wade through the chest-deep water, following his flashlight's narrow tunnel of light.

John breathed slowly and steadily to regulate his body temperature and steady his heart in the increasingly cold water. He wandered through the wet tunnel for a mile before hearing flapping wings in the darkness. He cut off his flashlight, took a deep breath, and submerged himself beneath the water. A shadow crossed overhead, a stryx flying inches from John's hiding place. John closed his eyes and prayed the creature away.

When he reopened his eyes, the stryx was gone. John surfaced, gasping for air. His flashlight flickered and the water dimmed its light, but it would have to do. There weren't enough flares to use them exclusively.

A long, slow hour passed as John trekked through the watery pathway to an intersection point. John checked

     Brock Enloe

the map one more time. Left led to the big cavern room and the Malus flower. Right wound toward the pit.

The flashlight faded to a faint glow and threatened to go out altogether. John tucked it away in his bag and struck a flare.

He'd only taken two steps toward the cavern room when the witch's cackle stopped him in his tracks. He dropped his arm into the water. The flare let out a quiet, brief hiss, and then the room was black. Then, something grabbed John's arm. Before he could scream, he was pulled behind a small cranny between several boulders.

John panicked and clenched his fists, trying to force his newfound abilities to kick in.

"Calm down."

The statement was terse and to the point. The voice was familiar. A lump formed in John's throat.

"Billy?"

Billy pulled John close and placed a hand over John's mouth. Nearby, something moved. The brothers squinted in the dark to see, but it was too dark even for shadows. But they felt a presence, the witch, move past them and meander down a tunnel.

John heard Billy's heart slow. "You're alive!"

"How did you get in here?" Billy asked.

"The Narrows," John whispered.

Billy's heart sped up. "So, there is a way out?"

"Yes." John reminded Billy to keep quiet. "But first I got to get the flower."

Billy let out a small laugh. "Turn your light on."

Billy waved the plastic container containing the Malus flowers.

"You still have them?" John asked.

"Let's get out of here, John."

John pushed a button on the side of his watch. His watch face lit up. It was three forty-five, three hours until sunrise.

"We can't leave now, or we won't make it home," John said. "Strigoi were circling the mountain at nightfall."

Billy shifted on the boulders for a comfortable position. "Okay, so what do we do?"

"We stay put here until at least five." John sighed. "Then, we make a run for it."

John settled onto a dry spot and handed Billy a water and granola bar. Billy carefully unwrapped both.

"I wanted to come back," John said. "I should've come back."

"It's okay," Billy said through a mouthful of granola bar, "you're here now."

John listened as Billy guzzled water. "I can't believe you're alive."

"I'm surprised, too." Billy washed down a bite of granola bar. "I hit water at the bottom of the pit and got carried off by the current, but not before those things took some chunks out of me."

"You got bit?"

"And slashed by their talons. I was freaking out and didn't know what to do. I dove under the water and started swimming and eventually wound up here. Been hiding here ever since."

John asked why he didn't try to escape.

"Look around, little brother—it's dark! Plus, every time I built up the courage, that witch thing would pass

     Brock Enloe

by cackling. It's like she knows I'm down here."

Despite the damp cold, John's face warmed with guilt. "Alright," he said boldly, "here's the plan."

***

Outside of the cave, day was dawning. Inside, John and Billy shivered in chilly water, only two turns from where The Narrows filtered out to the rest of the world.

John held up a hand and motioned for Billy to turn around. He whispered to answer the question on Billy's face. "I feel something ahead. We have to go a different way—through the boarded-up entrance."

They passed through the tunnels and waded closer to the abyss. John's flashlight gave off a weakening beam of light. They would need more to get across the pit. John passed his dying flashlight to Billy and dug a flare out of his bag. The red light came to life and brightened the tunnel, but John immediately doused it in water.

"Stay close," he whispered, looking up, "and keep the light pointed down."

Billy pointed his flashlight up, where three strigoi hung from the ceiling. Unnaturally large heads capped off the creatures' emaciated bodies and nearly touched the water. John and Billy sank deeper into the water and shuffled under the strigoi, holding their breath. They stared at the blood-soaked fangs and felt the tickle of warm, moist gusts of air as the monsters exhaled.

Around the corner and out of sight, John struck another flare. "Almost there," he mouthed.

A few minutes later, the brothers stood at the base of

the pit, staring up at the climb before them. John kicked something soft. He pointed his flare down to see the end of the rope.

"Alright, let's try this again." He offered the rope to Billy. "Sure you can make it up?"

Billy grabbed the rope. "I'll be fine."

John turned and stared down the tunnel behind him. Nothing but darkness. "Man," he said to himself, "déjà vu."

When John turned back around, Billy was at the top, pulling himself over the ledge. John grabbed the rope and began to climb. The cold water had taken a lot out of him, but the thought of getting out gave him a surge of adrenaline. He put one hand over the other and worked his way steadily up the rope.

He was twenty feet from the top when Billy called out.

"Hurry up, John!"

John shook his head and kept climbing.

"John!"

"I'm coming, Billy."

"Hurry up!"

John pulled himself up another couple feet. "You think I'm trying to go slow?"

"John, I need you, man!" Billy's voice quivered. "I got a stryx up here with me!"

As if to confirm the statement, the stryx let out a hoarse screech. John looked up. Billy's head hung off the edge of the pit. John gritted his teeth and pulled himself higher to see the stryx standing over Billy, straddling his body.

        Brock Enloe

John swung his left leg over the top of the cliff and landed it right beside Billy's head. Billy snatched a stake from John's makeshift leg holster and lunged up toward the stryx. The beast screeched as it tumbled over Billy and fell into the abyss.

Billy grabbed John's arm and pulled him to his feet. "Let's go!"

They sprinted away from the pit, their feet slapping against the hard ground. The cave entrance came into view, but there was no sunlight.

"Dude," Billy shouted, "you said the sun would be up by now!"

John ran beside Billy. "Sue me, man! How was I supposed to know the sun rises on the other side of the mountain?"

The boys raced out of the cave and kept running along the tracks around the bend. The morning sun beamed down on the other side of the bridge.

"Come on," John hollered. "We're almost to the light!"

The boys pumped their arms hard and started across the bridge.

"John!"

Two salivating strigoi swooped down and slammed onto the bridge, blocking the brothers from the sunlight. John and Billy turned to flee back toward the cave and came face to face with two more strigoi walking toward them.

"What now?" Billy cried out. "We're pinched! Can we wait for the sun to get here?"

The panting strigoi snarled and closed in on them.

"No time," John said. "We got to jump!"

"We gotta what?"

"You heard me!" John yelled. "We're gonna *Lost Boys* this junk!"

Billy looked over the edge, as the strigoi crept closer. "Dude, we'll die from that fall."

John took off his backpack and jacket. A parachute was strapped to his back. He handed a harness to Billy. "Buckle in!"

"Don't tell me that came out of that box we found in storage. Jimmy's grandad was in World War Two! This is forty years old!"

John smirked. "Are you coming or not?"

"We are so dead," Billy said, slipping the harness around his shoulders and buckling into the carabiner dangling from John's side.

"Vampires can't die from falling," John said, "right?"

"Yeah, but—"

John leapt from the iron bridge, pulling his brother into a free fall that Billy thought would never end. John searched for the ripcord, as he and Billy tumbled toward the treetops. He grabbed a loop and yanked hard. The old parachute spit out the pack, jerking the boys upward, out of the darkness and into the safety of the light.

The warm morning sun struck their faces as the strigoi let out a screech of defeat.

"Woohoo!" John flailed his arms around with joy.

Billy held tight to John, untrusting of the aged equipment. "Let's go!"

     Brock Enloe

# CHAPTER 12

# THE MULLIGAN

Cassie looked out at the morning sun. She was the only person awake inside The Roost. Fearing the worst, she opened the note from John and read it by the window in the growing sunlight.

Dear Cassie,

I hope you know that it was never my intention to hurt you. I'm sorry that I didn't tell you, and that you found out in the manner you did. The minute I found out about it, I wanted to tell you. I had to tell you, but then I couldn't. I just...it doesn't matter now. I should've told you from the very beginning.

I know it doesn't seem like it now, but I'm doing this because of you. Yes, I can't let my brother's death be in vain, but deep down it's my own selfish desires that brought me back into the mountain. I believe I can make things right between us. I desperately want to be with you, so that means I have to break this curse.

Ever since I laid eyes on you that day at the lake, I wanted to know you. I began asking Shane and Jimmy about you, even though they told me I had no shot. But it didn't matter, because I felt the way you looked at me that day.

Not shortly after that, I began blowing all of my money on pretzels at the drive in, just so I could see you. I got so tired of pretzels, but we began to talk more and more with every pretzel I ordered.

Then summer ended and school rolled around, and I signed up for all honors courses, hoping to be in some classes with you. The first day went by and I had no luck—until you walked in late to Honors History.

Then the night of the bonfire, we had our first kiss. I thought the universe was finally getting things right. But then I was attacked, and everything changed.

And lastly, the festival in Newburg. The night you told me you loved me. I remember that night as clear as day. I said you were all I needed, and that statement still holds true. But I said something that night that was a lie. I said if these were the last days of my life, I would be okay with that. That was far from the truth.

Since you told me you loved me, I realized that I have everything I could ever want. And now this curse threatens to take it all away.

The stryx has taken my brother, but I'll be danged if it takes you, too. Siting and dwelling on everything, the clearer it became that I had to find another way to the flower.

So, as you read this, just know that I'm so sorry for everything. I want you. I need you. And I love you. Don't worry about me. I'll be back soon.

After all, we still have that history project to present for Mr. Buckles class, remember? You're my partner, and I ain't about to let you present it alone.

I love you!

Love,

John

Cassie pressed the letter against her chest and sobbed, not knowing that John and Billy were gliding to safety.

The brothers stared down at the kids flooding into Burdine High just before the eight o'clock bell rang. They floated past downtown, sinking out of the sky and toward the field behind their house.

"Alright bro," John said, "this may hurt."

Their feet touched ground, and the brothers try to run to a stop, but the parachute tugged them forward. They tumbled to the ground, flipping and rolling to a painful halt.

"Ouch!" Billy disconnected his harness from John.

"We didn't die!" John cried.

Billy held up the flower. "Let's get to The Roost."

As they approached The Roost, the front door swung open.

"I thought you were dead!" Cassie held her arms out toward John.

"I told you I'd be back." John hugged her tightly. "Didn't you get the note I left for you?"

Cassie buried her head in John's shoulder.

"Cassie, I'm sorry," John stammered. "I should've—"

Cassie rested a finger on John's lips. "I'm just glad you're okay."

John watched as Cassie walked back into The Roost and called out for everyone to wake up. "So, are we okay?" he asked. "Would it help if I brought flowers? I mean, technically I did, but..."

"I'm happy you made it back with the flower," Cassie answered softly.

"You found the flower?" Shane wiped the sleep from his eyes.

"No, he didn't," Billy said, walking into The Roost. "I did."

"Dude, what?" Shane's mouth dropped open. "You're alive? You're alive!"

"I couldn't let your brother theory be right!" Billy laughed as Shane and Jimmy gave him bro hugs. Then, his laughter cut off abruptly. He pushed Shane and Jimmy away and approached Rachel, who was crying in disbelief.

She hopped off the ground for a big hug and an uncomfortable amount of kisses.

"Uh, Billy, Rachel—we're here," Shane said. "You know that, right?"

Neither Billy nor Rachel answered.

Once the passionate reunion ended, John and Billy

     Brock Enloe

gave a play-by-play of what happened in the cave. The others sat in silence, letting the insanity of their story sink in.

"There's something else." John sat on the couch. He leaned forward and scratched his face. "If me and Billy are gonna get cured completely, we have to work together, which means no more secrets."

Cassie locked eyes with John and raised an eyebrow.

"We have the flower, so Billy and I can drink the Malus remedy and get a few months of humanity back," John continued. "However, the medicine man whispered two things in my ear that night."

Cassie's eyebrows crept higher up her forehead.

"Number one," John said, "in order to break the curse completely, we have to kill the Shahidi."

"Kill the what?" Shane asked.

"That's exactly how I responded," Billy joked.

"Shahidi." John's voice was even, emotionless. "It's a Native American term meaning witch."

Jimmy rubbed his arms. "And is this what you guys saw down there?"

"Yeah," Billy said.

Cassie asked about the second thing the medicine man said.

John paused and tilted his head left and then right. "He said that the stryx that attacked me will continue to stalk me until one of us—either me or it—is dead."

"No way!" Shane shook his head. "Like a death pact or something?"

"What did it look like?" Rachel asked. "Would you recognize it?"

"It was big," John said, "bigger than any stryx I've seen since. And it had a scar across its face. Y'all were there that night, I'm sure you remember what it looks like."

"Not really," Shane said. "I just remember beaming it with a rock, and that thing got pissed!"

"What about the stryx we ran into on the way back from the festival in Newburg. Was it the same one that attacked you?" Cassie asked.

"Uh, not sure," John said. "I didn't get a good look at it."

"What about the one in the cave," Billy said, "the one that dug its talons into you when you jumped off the rock island?"

"I didn't jump off the island. That thing pushed me off. But I didn't get a good look at that one either."

Something sounded overhead. Footsteps scurried across the roof of The Roost. Shane and Billy leapt to their feet. The others sat still, listening intently. Then, John laughed softly.

"Just a squirrel," he said. "And yeah, maybe the medicine man was right. Maybe that creature is stalking me. But it doesn't matter. We just need to kill this witch, and then the curse is broken."

The sounds on the roof intensified. Now there were two, maybe three or more squirrels chasing each other, back and forth.

"Idea," Shane said. "Why not just sneak into the cave every four months and get another flower?"

"You haven't been down there." Billy rubbed Rachel's hand. "We were lucky to make it out of there alive with

     Brock Enloe

the flower once. Do that every four months? I don't think so."

"Well," Jimmy said slowly to keep his voice from shaking, "we want to help."

"Let's kill a witch!" Shane slammed a fist on the coffee table.

"Better plan," John said. "Can we just be normal high schoolers for a week?"

***

At the Daggon house, John made a special batch of Malus tea while Billy showered. Ten minutes later, Billy entered the kitchen wearing nothing but a pair of shorts. His chiseled body featured haphazard slashes, cuts, and bite wounds.

John held a steaming mug toward his brother. "Come on, bro, let's get this over with."

Billy took the mug and smelled its contents. "You couldn't have added some cinnamon or something?"

The brothers held their noses, counted to three, and chugged.

"Ugh!" John distorted his face in disgust.

Billy shrugged. "I've had worse."

"You're crazy! That stuff is..." John filled his coffee mug with water and washed down the remedy tea. "I'm going to shower."

When he returned to the kitchen a few minutes later, he wore sweatpants, a necklace, and a smile. "Yo, I can see myself again!" he shouted. "I showed up in the mirror—that stuff worked!"

Cassie grinned and pointed at the cross dangling from John's neck.

"I put it on before I went back into the mountain, and I've been wearing it since." John patted the necklace. "I think it's good luck."

***

Class presentations were the next day. Instead of letting the students choose when to go, Mr. Buckles dropped all the names in a glass jar.

Cassie gave John a knowing look. "We haven't even started."

"I'm sure our names won't get drawn first," John replied. "They can't."

Meanwhile, Mr. Buckles flitted his hand inside the jar and grabbed a slip of paper. "Okay, first group to present will be..." He unfolded the paper and held it at arm's length. "John Daggon."

John slid down into his desk chair.

"And John, your partner is Cassie Mentz, correct?" Mr. Buckles nodded at Cassie. "You guys will be presenting first thing tomorrow. We look forward to hearing what you have prepared."

Cassie grabbed John's arm as the bell rang. "What are we going to do?"

"Good question." John slung his backpack over his shoulder. "I can't work on it right now. I have basketball practice."

"Basketball practice? I thought you were suspended."

"Nope. Coach worked his magic, and my suspension

has been cut short. He told me this morning I'm cleared to play Thursday."

Cassie pursed her lips and crossed her arms.

"Don't worry! We can work on it after practice," John said. "Let's meet at The Roost."

"I don't think that's a good idea."

"Cassie—look I know you're still upset with me, but we're just going to work on the project. Then I'll drop you off afterward. Fair?"

Cassie thought a moment, then agreed. "I'll grab a few library books and wait for you at The Roost. But," she said with a huff, "I'll drive myself home."

John thought he saw steam rising from Cassie's head as she stomped away. "Sheesh." He was met with more heat inside the gym.

"Daggon, you're late!" Coach banged a finger against his wristwatch. "Since you and your brother missed practice yesterday without a doctor's note, you guys got a two-mile run before practice. Go!"

*** 

"Sorry, I'm late." John slammed The Roost door closed and tossed his bag on the couch.

"It's okay," Cassie groaned, her eyes glued to her history book. "This is going to be a nightmare tomorrow!"

"It's going to be okay," John promised. "I brought pizza—your favorite, alfredo cheese."

"How are you not worried sick over this?"

John dropped the pizza to the coffee table. "Um, I don't know." He grabbed a slice of pizza with one hand

and used the other to grab his history book from his backpack. "Maybe because over the past week I killed a stryx, wandered into a cave filled with danger, eluded death on multiple occasions, and jumped off a six-hundred-foot-tall bridge. Suddenly, a fifteen-minute presentation on World War Two doesn't seem that scary."

Cassie marked her place in her book and sighed. "I guess you have a point."

"And you," he said, "need a slice of this killer pizza."

It was nearly dark when they finished the project. John teased Cassie about her fears that he would try to make the evening romantic. "It was just a group project," he said, "nothing more."

"Fine, fine," Cassie said. "You were right."

"And to make the presentation even better, we'll bring an artifact!" John pointed at the parachute, which lay in a ball nearby. "And, uh—what are you doing?"

"Your fangs—they're gone!" Cassie held John's face and pushed out her lower lip. "I got to admit, they were growing on me. They were kind of hot."

"Oh, whatever." John pulled away from Cassie.

Cassie bit her lip. "I still think you're super cute, even if you just have normal human teeth."

Placing his hand on her face, John breathed in Cassie's strawberry lip gloss. Their lips closed in and nearly touched before Cassie pulled back slightly.

"I'm sorry," she said. "I just... I should go."

***

Cassie is still distant, but I get it. I just hope

          Brock Enloe

she comes around eventually, because I really do love her. As crazy as it sounds, I'm happy things played out the way they did. Sometimes you have to lose it all in order to gain everything.

Billy and I drank the Malus remedy, and it worked. However, I'm still nervous. We have a long way to

Billy slapped the journal out of John's hand. "Put it up, bro! Let's talk!"

"About what?" John picked up the journal and slid it under his bed.

"The witch." Billy sat on the edge of John's bed. "You think it's going to be hard to kill?"

John shrugged.

"What's the matter, John? We got to do this. We can't act like everything's normal until everything *is* normal."

"Twenty-four hours ago, I thought you were dead. Cassie left, Jimmy was mad, and the whole group split." John lowered his head and his voice. "I just got you back. All I want is normal."

Billy rubbed his hands together, looking for an answer.

"I'm not asking for a lot," John said. "Let's just take the rest of this week, enjoy what we have. Then Friday night, we camp out at The Roost and figure out how to off the witch."

Billy rubbed his chin thoughtfully. "We did promise Shane we would see *Halloween 4* once we got the flower."

* * *

Wednesday came and went. Somehow, Cassie and John got As on their presentation. The next day, Darrell Beckett stood in front of the class alone. He fidgeted with his hands and cleared his throat four times before getting started.

"It will be just me presenting today, because my partner is not here. But like Mr. Buckles stated, my topic is the Salem Witch Trials."

John perked up at the topic and flipped open a notebook to take notes.

Darrell explained that the trials started in 1692 and lasted a little over a year. More than two hundred were accused of being witches and thirty were found guilty. "While you may think this was a time when thousands were killed for being witches," Darrell said, "only nineteen were executed by hanging."

John strained to hear every detail and scribbled as much information as he could, hoping to find some crumb of data that could help with his impending witch battle.

"What did we learn from this historical event?" Darrell cleared his throat again. "I—I, I learned several things." He turned to the next page in his notes. "The first is that the colonists had no idea how to properly kill a witch."

A popping sound accented the end of his sentence. It was the intercom. Mrs. Warren, the school secretary, was all business.

*All members of the men's basketball team, please report out front. The bus leaves in ten minutes for the road game. Good luck boys, make us proud!*

Mr. Buckles told John he was free to leave.

"Actually," John said, "I think I'll stay for the rest of Darrell's presentation, if that's okay."

Mr. Buckles gave John a fatherly look of pride, then encouraged Darrell to continue.

"Um, yes—yessir." Darrell looked back down at his crumpled notes. "As I was saying, the colonists didn't know how to kill a witch properly, because they thought every witch was the same. You see, there are several species of witches, and each species has their own weaknesses and their own specific way that they must be killed. If a witch isn't killed in the proper way, it'll return and be stronger than before."

John's hand shot up. "So," he began, not waiting to be called on, "how do you identify the species of a witch?"

"Well," Darrell started, "they would have to—"

*John Daggon, please report to the front. The bus is waiting on you. John Daggon, to the front.*

John packed his things with a grumble and turned to Cassie. "Take notes," he pleaded. Then he walked out of the room.

# CHAPTER 13

# BECKETT CALL

I convinced Billy and the group to take the week off from everything, and it was a relaxing week until Darrell Beckett presented his history project on the Salem Witch Trials. I always heard that the universe gives you exactly what you need, the exact moment you need it.

John laughed and closed his journal as Billy entered their bedroom.

"What's up, dude?" Billy said. "How come you didn't come with us to the drive-in? You know, celebrate the win with a pretzel and see Cassie in her cute little uniform."

John grabbed the basketball from the floor and tossed it into the air. "Yeah, she doesn't really care to see me. Not anymore."

"I don't buy that one bit." Billy snagged the basketball out of the air. "What's going on?"

John explained that Cassie found the secret file about her dad and was upset that John kept it a secret.

"But you left her that letter," Billy said. "She said it was sweet."

John took the ball back and spun it in his hands. "Still doesn't change anything though. I hid all that information from her."

Billy tried to write it off and insisted Cassie would come around.

John hoped Billy was right. He fell back in his bed and shot the basketball toward the ceiling. "You know Darrell Beckett?"

"The short, weird kid with glasses?"

John sat up. "He ain't weird, bro. Just a little nerdy."

"What about him?"

"He gave a presentation today," John said.

"And?" Billy said.

"It was on the Salem Witch Trials."

"Whoa!" Billy sat on the edge of his bed. "Why am I just hearing about this?"

John tossed the ball in the air. "He said that there are different types of witches, and you gotta kill each one a specific way. Otherwise, the witch'll return and be more powerful than before."

"Well, how do you know what kind of witch you're dealing with?" Billy asked.

"I asked him that same question."

"And?"

"And then I got called out of class," John said, "to get on the bus for the game."

Billy pushed off his bed and stood in front of the

window overlooking the front yard. "We need to talk with Darrell."

***

Shane slammed his tray down on the cafeteria table. "Who serves mystery meat on Friday?"

Billy laughed.

John frowned. "Glad you're here," he said. "We've got plans."

"Don't tell me you guys are backing out." Shane shoved a forkful of mystery meat into his mouth and swallowed it without chewing. "We've been planning on seeing *Halloween 4* forever!"

"I think we should invite Darrell Beckett to The Roost this weekend," John said quickly.

Shane spewed his drink out of his mouth. "Uh, absolutely not!"

"Why not?" John asked.

"The dude is a total nerd," Shane said.

"Darrell's a nerd? We're nerds, man!" John's frown deepened. "We spent all of fall break hunting vampire-like creatures."

"I have to agree with Shane," Jimmy said. "Dude is weird, a total nerd."

"He knows a lot about witches," John said. "His presentation was on the Salem Witch Trials."

"So, you want to build your witch-killing plans off of Darrell Beckett's history project?" Shane laughed through a mouthful of cafeteria food. "Are you even listening to yourself right now?"

"John's right." Cassie said. "Darrell's project was very informative. I think he can help us, and he won't think we're weird for asking all about witches."

"I'm telling you," Jimmy said, "he's—"

"Listen," Billy said, cutting off Jimmy, "give the dude a chance. I don't care what he is if he can help us."

Rachel stabbed her fork into an orange gelatin cube. "I agree with the brothers. If Darrell can help, we have to try."

***

Unfortunately, getting Darrell to show up at The Roost was going to be harder than expected. He was a no-show in history class. Apparently, he got called into work, and his parents gave him permission to leave school early since his project was finished. Seemed odd to John, but Burdine was a small town, where that kind of stuff happened.

"I was going to give Darrell his grade today, but—" Mr. Buckles closed the door and walked to his podium.

"I'll take it, sir."

"That would be great, John! Don't want him worrying about his grade all weekend." Mr. Buckles walked to the back of the room and handed a folded paper to John. "He works at the comic book shop downtown. And no peeking at his grade."

"Aye, captain." John raised a hand to his forehead. "No peeking—got it!"

John zoned out as the next group started their presentation. He wondered what Darrell would think when he walked through the doors at the comic shop. Then he considered whether he still had a chance with Cassie. They almost kissed a few nights before, but she was still acting differently. Did she want to talk about the situation? John didn't know what he would say to make things better.

His thoughts returned to the classroom when a piece of paper slapped onto his desk. John flipped it over and saw Cassie's sleek cursive. He peeked her direction, but she was facing forward.

> *I'll ride with you to give Darrell his grade. Are we going right after school?*

John grinned, then clicked the button on his pen.

> Thanks! And yeah, I'll get Shane to take Billy home and then you and I can take The Fury to go talk with Darrell.

John folded the paper and tossed it onto Cassie's desk when Mr. Buckles wasn't looking. When the bell rang, he approached Cassie. "Ready to go?"

"Yep."

Shane, Billy, and Jimmy were already in the parking lot, waiting.

"There he is!" Shane shouted. "You ready to grab a snack and chill at The Roost until movie time?"

"Actually, Cassie and I need to run an errand. Billy," John said, "you mind riding home with Shane and letting me take The Fury?"

Billy held the keys toward John on one finger. "How'd the talk with Darrell go?"

          Brock Enloe

"He wasn't in class." John took the keys. "He left for work early. Meet you guys at The Roost before the movie."

"Wait, where does he work?" Jimmy asked.

Cassie opened The Fury's passenger door and said, "The comic book shop."

"I told you, bro!" Shane doubled over with laughter. "He is such a nerd!"

The ride was quiet and awkward, but John broke the tension by thanking Cassie for joining him on the trip.

"You'd do the same for me," Cassie uttered. "Plus, I figured you can't hide any information from me if I stay by your side."

"Ouch!" John winced. "I guess I deserve that, but I really am sorry. You know that, right?"

Cassie looked out the window and tucked her hair behind her ears. "You think Darrell can really help?"

"Cassie, come on!" John hit his palm against the steering wheel. "Don't change the subject. I'm sorry that I hurt you. I wish I could go back in time and do it differently. I made a mistake, but I'm trying here. I mean, I don't know what else to say, but...I love you."

Cassie swallowed the lump in her throat as they passed under a large tree with flaming-orange leaves that leaned over the street. "I'm trying too. I mean I'm here, aren't I? I want us to work, and I want to be with you, but..." Tears built in her eyes. "I just need time."

John popped open the glove box and grabbed a small stack of tissues. He handed one to Cassie and turned up the radio. They cruised toward downtown with Bryan Adams's "Heaven" serving as their soundtrack. As the song came to a close, John whipped The Fury into a tight parking spot and shut off the engine.

The shops were decorated for Halloween, pumpkins were squeezed into every available space, and the fall leaves rustled across the street.

"I don't come downtown very often," Cassie said. "I forgot how pretty it is, especially this time of year."

"You think this is pretty?" John pushed open the front door to the comic shop. "You should see the view from above."

The comic shop smelled of old paper and stale air. A voice called out from the back of the shop, "I'll be right out!"

Cassie and John browsed the aisles as they waited. John dug through a used comic bin.

"John Daggon, I didn't know you were a comic book guy." Darrell held a box of comic books.

John shrugged. "I dabble occasionally."

"Well, you're in luck!" Darrell's eyes lit up. "We just got a big shipment in today. New *Watchmen*, *Fantastic Four*, *Daredevil*, *Swamp Thing*—even got a couple new *Spiderman* comics in."

"Oh, wow!" Cassie faked excitement. "You really got it all, huh?"

"Sure do!" Darrell set the box down on the front countertop. "But what are y'all searching for?"

"Actually," John said, "we're looking for two things."

"Okay, shoot!" Darrell said cheerfully.

"First off, Mr. Buckles asked us to drop this off to you." John handed over the paper with Darrell's project grade. "He didn't want you stressing over your grade."



Brock Enloe

Darrell unfolded the paper and gave it a quick, unimpressed look. "You didn't come here for this. Do you even like comics?"

Cassie tried to act interested in comics. Thankfully, John didn't make her work at it for long.

"You know a lot about witches. I was hoping maybe you could tell us more on the subject."

"So, you're not into comics," Darrell said. "You're into witches. Let's talk Monday, at lunch."

"I was hoping we could talk tonight—if you're up for it," John said. "We're having a sleepover at my house, and I thought maybe you'd be up for hanging out and talking witches?"

"Man, I appreciate the offer, really! Sadly, Dad—a.k.a. my boss—wants the new inventory on the shelf by Monday." Darrell patted the box of comics. "This will take me all weekend."

"That is a lot of comics," John said.

"Yeah," Cassie butted in, "but what if we helped put the inventory out?"

"You'd do that?"

"Yeah, man! Think we could get it out before seven tonight?" John asked. "We're going to see the new *Halloween* movie before the sleepover."

"Oh, dude—yes!" Darrell raised his right hand, as if holding a knife like Michael Myers. I'll call Dad after the inventory is out and let him know I'm hanging with you guys!"

***

John threw The Fury in park and hopped out shouting, "Yes Shane, I know we're running late! I just have to change clothes, and then we can all leave."

Shane hurried after John, following him into the Daggon house. "What is he doing here?"

"Oh, Darrell?" John moved through the hallway to his bedroom. "He's going to the movies with us, then staying the night at The Roost."

"It was supposed to be a chill night, dude."

John pulled a shirt over his head. "It's gonna be, promise." John slapped Shane on the shoulder and walked out of his room. "We just spent three hours together, putting away comic books. I think you'll like him."

When John and Shane walked out of the house, Jimmy hollered. "Yo, Shane—this dude is awesome! He brought a whole box of comics for us."

"No way!" Shane said. "Let me see!"

"And Shane," Jimmy said with a wink, "there are a couple Batman in here, too."

John walked to Billy and smirked. "And Shane said Darrell was the nerd?"

John, Billy, Cassie, and Rachel led the two-car caravan. Shane, Jimmy, and Darrell brought up the rear.

"Five minutes ago, Shane was upset Darrell was here," John said, "but now that Darrell brought Batman comics, they're best friends."

Billy caught John's eye in the rearview mirror. "I'm just glad that they're getting along. If we want a shot at killing this witch, we need everybody."

"Enough witch talk for now," John said. "Let's enjoy the movie."

     Brock Enloe

"You're right, John. Speaking of enjoying"—Billy winked at Rachel—"let's grab seats on the back row."

The group rushed into the theater, and John grabbed popcorn, drinks, and candy. He handed a package of peanut M&Ms and a ticket to Cassie.

"My favorite!" Cassie smiled. "How'd you know?"

"Because I know you."

Cassie opened the candy and rolled a single M&M out. "Thanks for the snacks and for the movie ticket."

"I'm just glad you still wanted to sit with me," John said with a flirtatious grin.

"Yeah, don't read into it too much." Cassie looked at her ticket. "And back-row seats?"

John blushed. "The rest of the theater is full. Besides, the seats are better back there. The view is, too. You don't have to strain your neck looking up the whole time."

"Right." Cassie brushed past John to find a seat. "You prefer back-row seats so your neck doesn't hurt."

For two hours, the real threat of witches and strigoi took the back seat, as a make-believe killer slashed one victim after another on the screen. Jimmy, Shane, and Darrell hid behind their hands, laughing nervously and screaming at every jump scare. Billy and Rachel spent half the movie with their faces glued together. John and Cassie spent most of the movie awkwardly bumping hands in the popcorn bag.

During a particularly intense scene, Cassie gave in and leaned on John's shoulder and squeezed his arm. While he couldn't hear Cassie's heart, John suspected it was moving as fast as his own.

As they exited the theater, Rachel was the first to

realize they made a mistake. "How are we going to get to The Roost? It's so dark."

"We'll drive to the wood line behind the house," Billy said, "and then all move together quickly."

"You guys scared of the dark or something?" Darrell chewed on his last Raisinet and tossed the empty box in a trashcan.

"Wait." Jimmy sneered at Darrell's choice of candy. "What about the pizza?"

"You're really worried about pizza?" John uttered. "With all we have going on?"

Jimmy looked from face to face for some sympathy. "No, I mean, I just know we'll get hungry later."

"Fine, I'll swing by and pick up pizza." John scratched his neck. "You guys park at the wood line and wait on us!"

"Do not get out of the car," Billy said sternly. "Not until all of us are there. We go together."

***

Yellow headlights cut through the tree line. Jimmy sat in the driver's seat of his mom's station wagon, with the car running and the windows up. Shane and Darrell looked outside with visions of *Halloween 4* dancing in their heads.

"So, what are we doing all the way back here?" Darrell asked.

"The Roost is a couple hundred yards through the woods," Jimmy said. "We pretty much crash here every weekend."

A shadow bobbed ahead. Shane tensed up, then relaxed. It was a tree branch swaying in the wind.

"Why's everyone so worried?" Darrell said. "What's the big deal about getting here at night?"

The conversation was cut short by a rumbling and a honk. John pulled The Fury beside the wagon and rolled down his window slightly. "Everybody got something? We can't leave anything behind."

"We've got it," Shane promised.

John rolled his window back up and gave the signal to get moving. The doors to both cars popped open simultaneously. Hands reached for items, then feet followed after Billy, who carried a flashlight in one hand and a flare in the other. Weaving between boulders and ducking under the drooping limbs, the group wandered deeper into the darkness.

At the clearing, Billy motioned for everyone to get down. He held one finger to his lips. "I heard something."

"We are almost there," John said. "Keep moving!"

"Okay." Billy rested on his hands and knees. "As soon as we pass through the shrubbery and enter the clearing, I'll send up a flare. Once I fire it, we sprint to The Roost. Understand?"

Six silhouetted heads nodded in agreement.

"Let's go!"

With that, the group sprinted forward, only to have the wood's dense vegetation slow their progress.

"This stuff's like molasses," Shane said. "We're like sitting ducks out here."

"Now!" Billy fired the flare into the sky, turning the forest a bright red, then grabbed Rachel's arm and pulled her forward as he sprinted through the woods.

Billy's heart pounded in his chest as he flung The Roost door open. Rachel, Shane, Cassie, and Jimmy tumbled inside.

"Where's John?" Billy asked. He looked into the woods, where John ran back for Darrell, who was on the ground.

"Where's my bag?" Darrell shouted. "I can't see it!"

"Guys, come on!" Billy called. "The flare's gone. You shouldn't be out there this lo—"

A petrifying screech rattled through the trees.

John held something up in the darkness. "It's right here—let's go!"

"Come on, guys! Hurry!" Cassie watched from The Roost, paralyzed with fear.

John pushed Darrell, pleading for him to run faster as the flap of a stryx's wings closed in on them.

Shane tried to push past Billy at the door. "They aren't gonna make it!"

"Yes, they are." Billy held his arms across the doorframe, keeping Shane inside The Roost. "They got this. Come on, John. Come on, John..."

The screeching grew louder and louder. Billy flung Shane to the ground and took a step backward as John shoved Darrell into The Roost and dove over him. Billy slammed the door shut and locked it in one motion.

The winged creature stared at them through the window and growled. It bared its fangs, then disappeared into the night.

John went numb. "Did you see the scar on its face? That's the one that attacked me. It's the same one. It's

		Brock Enloe

following me! Billy, it's following me, it's following me!"

Billy dropped the curtain over the window.

"Are we safe?" Rachel whimpered.

"Safe as we can be," Billy said. "It can't come in. We'll be fine, and it'll be gone in the morning."

"Okay, wha—wha, wha…" Darrell's eyes bulged under his glasses. "What was that?"

# CHAPTER 14

# TAXONOMY

"You're saying that creature is a vampire?" Darrell pushed his glasses up on his nose.

"Not a vampire," John said. "A stryx."

"Which is a vampire-like creature," Shane said.

Darrell shivered. "And John was attacked by one and will transform into one, if we don't kill some witch in a cave?"

"Yes," Shane said. "Billy too! He was attacked also, and we actually thought he died for a short stint there, but then we, well, John—"

"Shut up!" Billy threw an empty soda bottle at Shane.

"Darrell, I should've told you sooner, but this is why we needed to talk with you. Your knowledge on witches could be the only thing that saves our lives." John touched his tongue to the tip of his canines. They were starting to grow again. "You don't have to help us kill the witch, we just need to know how to find it."

　　　　Brock Enloe

Darrell paced The Roost with his hands on his head, breathing heavily.

"Uh, Darrell, you okay?" Jimmy took a bite of pizza.

Darrell mumbled something to himself, then stopped his pacing and began to wipe his glasses off with his shirt tail. "Sorry, I, uh... You guys are the only people who have been nice to me, so—yeah, I'll help." He set his glasses back in place and gave a weak smile. "I can't have my only friends dying on me."

"Thanks, man." John sighed.

"No problem, and I'm helping kill that witch."

"Darrell," Billy started.

"I'm part of the group, right?" Darrell looked at each person, daring them to challenge his place in the group. "Shane said we look after each other no matter what. I'm part of that *we*."

"Of course you're part of the group," John said. "But you don't have to risk your life."

"You're one of us dude!" Shane yelled. "Let's kill us a witch!"

"For now," Jimmy said, "let's eat!"

John climbed halfway up the loft ladder. He held on with one hand and raised a slice of pepperoni pizza in the air with the other. "To the newest member of the group, Darrell Beckett. Sorry for almost getting you killed during your first night with us."

"To Darrell Beckett!"

As they celebrated, Darrell asked a series of questions. What was the witch's motivation? No one knew. What did it look like? Big, with long arms, stringy hair, and a cackle that would send shivers up a ghost's back. Darrell hung his head. The witch could be any species. With more than twenty possibilities, he needed more information.

"We have to find its coven," Darrell said, "its house. If we can see what's in there, we can narrow down the type of witch we're dealing with."

"Wait, you want us to go to this thing's house?" Shane rapped on the top of the coffee table. "Knock, knock, it's us! Tell us a little bit about yourself, if you don't mind."

"Any idea where its coven is?" Darrell asked.

John sat on the edge of the loft. "Both times we saw the witch, it was deep in the depths of the mountain."

"Oh, please!" Billy wiped pizza grease off his mouth. "Tell me we don't have to go back in there."

"Don't worry, it won't be inside the mountain," Darrell insisted. "Witches cast spells in their coven, and they need moonlight. No moonlight inside a mountain."

"Best news I heard all day," Jimmy mumbled.

"A witch's coven is usually—well, somewhere like out there." Darrell pointed to a window. "Deep in the woods, far away from pretty much everything."

A memory jostled around in John's brain. "Billy," he blurted out, "what about that hut we saw from the parachute?"

Billy moved his head from left to right. "It was deep in the woods," he admitted. "And it was beneath the far side of the mountain."

"Oh yeah?" Darrell finished a slice of pizza and took a sip of soda.

"Yeah," Billy said. "No driveway, no car, nothing. Just a small hut surrounded by wilderness."

"That definitely fits the description," Darrell said.

       Brock Enloe

"Well," John said, "looks like we're going exploring tomorrow."

***

Tomorrow came early for John. He sat up in his sleeping bag and checked his watch. Two forty-eight. But there was no going back to sleep. He was wide awake.

Resigned to staying awake the rest of the night, he stepped over his sleeping friends, grabbed a pen and paper, and mapped out every possible route to the coven, writing down the risks of each one. He was so focused on his work that he didn't hear Cassie's heartbeat until she sat down beside him.

"You still having nocturnal issues?"

"Just can't sleep," John said.

Cassie giggled quietly. "I think that classifies as a nocturnal issue."

"How about you—what are you doing up?" John asked. "Are you having nocturnal issues?"

"Figured you could use some company." She placed a hand on the map John had drawn. "Talk me through what you've got there."

John walked her through the options for accessing the coven, growing animated as he explained the potential dangers of each approach.

"Sounds like a good plan to me." Cassie scooted so close to John their sides almost touched.

"S-s-so," John stuttered, "you don't have any concerns with the plan?"

Cassie inched closer. "Uh-uh."

John gazed into Cassie's eyes, the plan all but forgotten. He brushed her hair out of her face and leaned in. Just before their lips meet, he paused and let out a small sigh. "I really want to kiss you right now, but not if it's going to make things more confusing."

"Ugh!" Cassie groaned. "You had to ruin it."

"I'm sorry! I just... I'm just confused. I don't want to mess this up—again." John ran a hand across his hand-drawn map. "I love you and want to be with you. I don't know what else you want me to say."

"Nothing. I want you to kiss me!"

"And I want to kiss you, but you said you needed time. And as badly as I want to kiss you right now," John said, "I won't do it if it means jeopardizing our relationship."

"I'm going back to bed." Cassie got to her feet with a huff. "Good night, John."

John tossed the pen onto the table and made his way back to his sleeping bag. He tossed from one side to the other trying to get comfortable. When he did, he locked eyes with Darrell.

"Should've kissed her," Darrell whispered.

"Good night, Darrell."

***

A few hours later, John told the plan while everyone else ate. There would be two teams. Team one—John, Billy, Shane, and Darrell—was going to the coven to gather information. Team two—Rachel, Cassie, and Jimmy—would hang back and assist with an escape if things went south.

"You take care of the girls, Jimmy! Anything happens," Billy said, "make sure they don't get hurt."

"Yes, sir," Jimmy replied with an overzealous salute.

"So, two teams," Shane said. "What's the plan after that?"

John explained that train tracks passed through downtown Burdine and went closer to the potential coven site than the decommissioned track they used with the railcar. When trains rode through town, they slowed down. Team one would hop on one and ride it around the lake and up a couple hundred yards into the woods. Then, they would bail at the abandoned campground.

From there, the plan was to take the hiking trail that led to where they believed the coven was. Once they found the coven, they would get the information needed, then hurry back down the mountain before dark.

Billy chugged a cup of coffee. "That's not a bad plan, but how are we getting back down the mountain and across the lake before nightfall?"

"We deflate the tube from Shane's boat and carry it up the mountain." John paused, expecting Shane or Billy or someone to interrupt. No one did. "Once we have what we need, we find the creek, inflate the tube, and let the rapids carry us back down to the lake, where team two will be waiting with Shane's boat."

"Sounds a little crazy." Shane picked a biscuit crumb from his shirt and licked it off his finger. "But, well, I don't have any better ideas."

"I mean, it could work," Billy said. "What do you think, Darrell? You know more about these witches than anyone. You okay with the plan?"

Darrell tugged at his shirt collar. "If you guys like the plan, then I like the plan."

"Girls," John said, "any thoughts?"

Cassie and Rachel looked at each other, then back at John and shook their heads.

"Well," John said, "there we have it. We move out after breakfast."

***

Smoke billowed from the train's chimney. Crisp October air swept across the boys' faces as they sat above the tracks. They tried to relax and enjoy the views as they neared the jump point. Red, orange, and yellow foliage engulfed them as they traveled deep into the woods. When they emerged from the wood line, the train picked up speed and raced alongside the lake.

"Grab your gear and hold it tight," John said. "We're about to bail."

"It's moving pretty fast," Darrell said, staring at the ground that blurred. "Are you guys sure about this?"

Shane strapped his backpack on. "You'll be okay, dude. Just aim for something soft."

"Okay," Billy said, "here we are! Three, two, one, JUMP!"

Billy and John tumbled to a stop and stood up to find Jimmy and Darrell.

"Dude, they're still on the train!" Billy exclaimed.

"Jump!" John shouted.

Shane put an arm around Darrell and leapt, pulling Darrell with him. The two of them braced for impact but came to a soft landing in a patch of grass. They rolled to a stop and laughed.

"Not so bad, right?" Shane said as he gathered his gear that fell out of his unzipped bag.

John and Billy ran to check on Shane and Darrell. "You guys okay?" John asked.

Shane gave a thumbs-up. Darrell straightened his glasses.

"You guys had me nervous," John said. "I thought you weren't going to jump."

Shane smirked. "Darrell was just really enjoying the train ride. He didn't want it to end."

Billy grabbed the straps of Darrell's backpack and used them to lift him to his feet. "You nailed that landing," he said. "Harrison Ford couldn't have made it look any better."

Darrell grinned and swiped a hand against his clothes to knock off grass and dirt.

"Hardest part is over now," Shane said.

Billy, Shane, and John started toward the woods, leaving Darrell behind, brushing himself off. "Come on Indiana Jones," Billy said, "we need you to identify this witch."

A heavy quietness blanketed the woods, putting the boys on edge.

"We need to check in with the others," John stated. He pulled out the walkie-talkie and resumed the hike. "Team two, come in! We have made the jump and have located the trail."

John dropped the walkie to his side and kept walking.

"Good deal!" Jimmy called through the walkie. "We

tied the boat off to a willow tree and will be waiting on you guys. Be safe and keep us in the loop."

"Will do, and you, too," John said. "Over and out."

Jimmy set the walkie down, closed his eyes, and kicked his feet up on the boat's dashboard.

"So," Rachel said to Cassie, "you're still not budging with John?"

"No, I mean—I have moments of weakness. Like we almost kissed last night, but..."

"But what?" Rachel asked.

"But John...he said he didn't want to kiss me if it meant risking our relationship."

"That makes no sense."

"No, he was right." Cassie dipped her hand in the lake. "I wanted to kiss him in the moment, but earlier that day, I told him I needed time. He was just trying to give me what I wanted."

A slight breeze blew across the lake. The boat rocked gently.

"If you don't want to be with him," Rachel said, "then why do you still defend him?"

Jimmy kept his eyes closed, and the girls pretended he wasn't there.

"I don't know," Cassie admitted. "I want to be with him, but I can't shake the feeling of betrayal, so I try to find a way to despise him. As bad as that sounds, I try to tell myself that I don't love him, that it was never real between us. Like, why didn't he show me the file? That's the part that hurts the most. If he really loved me, then he would have told me about my dad. Instead, he let me find that folder in his desk drawer."

     Brock Enloe

A lump formed in Jimmy's throat. He debated whether to jump in and tell Cassie the truth. That it was all his fault, not John's. Before he settled the debate, John called through the walkie-talkie.

Cassie and Rachel rushed to the back of the boat.

"We hear you," Jimmy said. "What's going on?"

"We have found the coven."

Jimmy, Cassie, and Rachel shared a look of concern. "Be safe, guys. It's four o'clock now," Jimmy said. "Sunset is in fifty minutes."

"I know, I know," John said quickly. "It took us longer than expected to find the coven. And we need something from you."

"Anything," Jimmy said.

"Until you hear from us, don't make contact. We don't know what we'll find in there," John said. "So, we need radio silence. Understand?"

Jimmy pressed the walkie against his forehead and mumbled, "Ten-four."

"One more thing." John's tone deepened. "If we aren't at the lake by sunset, get the girls out of there before darkness falls. Don't wait on us."

Rachel reached for the walkie-talkie, but Jimmy held it out at arm's length, where she couldn't grab it. "We have to," Jimmy told Rachel. Cassie pulled Rachel back to the front of the boat.

"Okay," Jimmy said into the walkie.

"Jimmy, we mean it." It was Billy. His voice bordered on anger. "Don't put the girls in danger because you want to wait on us."

"I understand," Jimmy said. "Leave by sunset no

matter what, and radio silence until we hear from you."

John turned off the walkie-talkie and stuffed it in his backpack. He gazed upon a rock-sculpted hut illuminated by the sinking sun.

"What's the plan?" Shane asked.

"We get Darrell to the window," John said, "so he can look inside."

"Great plan!" Shane gave a sarcastic smile.

"Whatever we do, we need to get a move on," Billy said. "It's already getting dark."

Billy and Shane maneuvered around the tree line and in front of the creek to keep watch, as John and Darrell crept toward the coven. Just outside the hut, John and Darrell crouched.

John peeked inside. "All clear," he mouthed to Darrell.

Darrell popped his head up. While he inspected the coven, John faced Shane and Billy, making sure nothing caught them by surprise in the darkening woods.

"We got to hurry, Darrell," John whispered.

"I can't see much." Darrell ducked back under the window. "I need to get inside."

"No way!" John said. "Are you crazy?"

"If you want to identify this witch, you'll help me get inside."

John rested his head against the hut. "Okay—move, move."

Darrell scooted away from the window, and John pressed his hands against the window and pushed it up.

Shane covered his mouth. "What are they doing?"

Darrell put a foot in John's hand, and John hoisted him up and over the wooden window sill.

        Brock Enloe

"Be quick," John whispered.

John crouched below the window again and listened to Darrell wander around inside.

"Pssst!" Billy waved his arms, trying to get John's attention. "Pssst!"

John held up his hands in confusion.

Billy crossed his arms in an X shape over his chest and mouthed, "Abort!" Shane pointed at something behind the hut. John snuck to the edge of the hut and looked to see an outlined figure moving swiftly. Its long, claw-like arms swung loose at its side, and its stringy hair bounced with every stride.

John scurried to the window. "We have to go—now!"

Darrell ran to the window and crawled out. John eased the window closed and turned to run. Before they took a step, they noticed Billy, wide-eyed with both hands held out toward them. John and Darrell crouched.

Behind them, smoke rose from the coven's chimney.

John and Darrell stared at Billy, frozen in fear as a burning scent flowed out of the coven. Billy instructed Shane to inflate the tube. Shane went to work, forcing every molecule of oxygen in his lungs into the tube. The darkness deepened.

John checked his watch. Four forty. "We got to make a run for it," he whispered to Darrell.

Darrell shook his head and the rest of his body.

John counted down with his fingers: Three, two, one. They stood up and peeked into the window. A pair of beady black eyes looked back at them.

The witch cackled, showing off a mouthful of pointy teeth before vanishing from the window.

"RUN!" John screamed.

Shane jumped at the noise and plugged the tube shut. He and Billy carried the raft through the woods and dropped it into the creek.

"Come on, come on, come on," Billy muttered.

John and Darrell weaved through the trees, hounded by the witch's long gait.

"Almost there!" John yelled.

John and Darrell tumbled down the wooded slope, picked themselves back up, and leapt off a boulder into the creek. Shane and Billy pulled them onto the tube and pushed away from the bank. The water deepened quickly, and the current rushed them away. The four stared back at the witch, who faded into the shadows.

Crammed onto the small tube, the boys were soaked by the frigid white foam that spewed up from the rapids.

"It's almost dark!" Billy said. "We need to contact the others."

John fought to stay balanced on the tube as he dug through his bag. When he found the walkie, he moaned. "It's completely soaked!"

"Try it anyway!" Shane shouted.

John raised the walkie to his purple lips as his teeth chatter. "Come in, guys! We are headed down the mountain now. I repeat, we are headed down the mountain."

Downstream, Jimmy started the boat motor. "They told me to get you out of here by dark, and that's what I am going to do."

"It's not even dark yet!" Rachel yelled.

"Look, I don't want to leave them either! They're my

friends!" Jimmy put the boat in gear. "But they told me to protect you."

"Wait!" Cassie grabbed the walkie and turned the volume all the way up. "Did you hear that?"

Jimmy killed the engine.

John's distorted voice broke over the walkie in fits and starts. "We...down...mountain...narrowly...witch..."

"We've got to wait. You heard them!" Cassie cried. "They're headed down the mountain!"

Jimmy cranked the boat engine. "I didn't hear nothing but some muffled noise and the word *witch*. They told me to keep you out of harm's way. The sun has set. As much as I want to stay and wait, we can't."

The girls stared up river, fighting back tears as Jimmy eased the boat back toward the launch ramp. Through the dusky, hazy light, a dark, four-headed blob came into view. Rachel jumped to her feet.

"There they are!" she shouted. "Turn around, Jimmy!"

***

"Alright, Darrell," John said, "what kind of witch are we dealing with here?"

"Not quite sure."

The group sat in Cassie's living room. Her mom was out of town for the night. John, Billy, Shane, and Darrell wore oversized, outdated clothing. Cassie snagged it from her dad's closet. While the outfits lacked style, they were dry. That was all that mattered.

"I thought seeing the witch's coven would help you identify its species." John said.

"It did," Darrell said. "Now, we have narrowed our witch down to three species: a Desahorax, Beautorax, or Myrtu-curier."

Darrell explained that the Desahorax is known as a witch of trickery. Though uncommon, this witch is very powerful. A Beautorax is commonly known as a seductress.

"Oh, please be the seductress witch," Shane said. "Please be the seductress witch."

"I hate to burst your bubble," John said, "but I was face to face with that witch. I can pretty much promise you that is not a seductress witch."

"And the last option?" Billy wrapped his arm around Rachel.

"The Myrtu-curier," Darrell said. "*Myrtu* means death. And the word *curier*, well that means carrier or deliverer."

John exhaled loudly. "The death deliverer?"

"Yes, the deliverer of death." Darrell tilted his head down and looked over his glasses. "Better known as the death witch."

"How do we narrow the species down to one?" Billy asked.

Darrell shrugged. "There's only one way I can think of, and you guys aren't going to like it."

# CHAPTER 15

# THE CONFIRMATION

Tomorrow night is Halloween, which happens to be the night of the Stygian moon—the darkest night of the year, according to my science textbook. But I'm not too concerned with science right now. Darrell said that on this night, the Myrtu-curier is the only witch known to visit its coven. So, no trick-or-treating this year. After the annual Halloween Hoops basketball game at 5:30, we go witch hunting.

I am a bit nervous about a night mission, since Billy fell into the pit and I lost Cassie during our last night mission. Looking on the bright side, we don't have to go inside the mountain, and Cassie isn't really talking to me, so I can't lose what I don't have.

John shoved a Scorpions cassette into his boombox

and hit play. Picking up his basketball, he lay on his bed and worked on his shooting form, repeatedly flicking his wrist and propelling the ball up in the air, over and over, as the music blasted through the room.

***

*Good evening and Happy Halloween! This is Carl Ables from 97.1 The Bruin, and sitting to my right is my cohost, Cecil Edwards. We are coming to you live on this Friday afternoon from the Burdine Bruins' home gym, better known as The Den! With fifteen minutes until tip off, I expect it to be a packed house here this evening for the annual Halloween Hoops game! What are your thoughts for tonight, Cecil?*

*What are you talking about, Carl? It's already a packed house in here! I can barely hear myself think and fans are still rolling in.*

*If they let many more in, they'll be breaking the fire code. But enough about that. Let's talk about this match up tonight: the Burdine Bruins versus the Pikeville High Pirates.*

*Usually, Pikeville wins this game, Carl, but I think Burdine fans are hopeful. I know the Pirates are a class-six team and the Bruins are class-four, but this season hasn't been typical for Burdine.*

Cassie and Rachel sat on the top bleacher, right behind Shane, Jimmy, and Darrell.

"You guys picked the worst possible seats," Shane joked. "We can barely see from up here."

Cassie looked at the back of Shane's head. "If you wanted better seats, you should have got here an hour ago."

"Sorry!" Jimmy said. "We had to pick up all the supplies for the mission."

"Yeah," Shane said. "You should be grateful."

"Thanks." Darrell turned around and smiled. "Thank you for saving us seats."

Cassie pretended to curtsy in a seated position. "You're welcome, Darrell."

"At least someone is appreciative of our efforts," Rachel said. "And yes, you're welcome, Darrell."

*The atmosphere is electric here, Carl! These fans must really believe Burdine has a chance to beat Pikeville this year.*

*Well, we've had enough speculation. It's time to find out. The tip is up and Burdine wins the jump ball. John Daggon brings the ball down the floor for the Bruins. He dumps the ball to his brother, Billy, who catches it at the high post. Billy gives a jab right before driving left. All the way to the rim, basket is good. Burdine up two to zero.*

The first half was a back-and-forth contest, surprising Pikeville and energizing the Burdine fan base. With a minute and a half left, Billy was benched due to foul trouble, but John kept the game from getting out of hand. Coach Jenkins called a time-out with twenty seconds left on the clock. Burdine was down by eight, the largest gap since the opening tipoff.

"Hold for the last shot, and try to cut into this lead

before half. Got it?" The coach set his whiteboard on his belly and began to draw a play. "Run twenty-two dice and look for John in the corner coming off the low screen."

*Alright, Cecil—let's see what the Bruins do right here before the half with Pikeville up fifty to forty-two with twenty seconds before the break. Burdine inbounds the ball. John Daggon dribbles up the floor and begins to kill time.*

*Looks like they are going to hold it for last shot. Not a bad call.*

*Ten seconds left. John swings it to Tommy on the left wing and runs right. Tommy pump-fakes and drives in. Six, five, four... Tommy stops and kicks out to the left corner, finding John coming off the screen. John catches. Shoots. It rolls around the rim and falls in. A big time three from John Daggon to cut the lead to five at the half!*

*Will you listen to that! The crowd loved that, Carl. We'll be back after the break. You're listening to 97.1 The Bruin.*

"We'll be right back, ladies," Jimmy said. "Going to get some snacks."

Rachel nodded and looked at Cassie, whose eyes were glued to John as he made his way toward the locker room.

"Still giving him the cold shoulder?" Rachel asked.

"Huh?"

Rachel laughed. "John. You still haven't talked with him?"

"Oh, no," Cassie stuttered. "No, not yet."

Rachel waved at a cluster of girls who were making

their way across the basketball court to the concession stand. "Well, Billy caught John listening to 'Still Loving You' by the Scorpions, so John is obviously still thinking about you."

A slight grin started on Cassie's face, as the boys climbed up the bleachers, empty-handed.

"Can you believe they were sold out of popcorn?" Jimmy grumbled. "Who sells out of popcorn at halftime?"

"Burdine High," Shane said, "that's who."

The girls shared an eye roll, letting their conversation end unfinished.

Burdine started the second half strong and fought back to regain the lead. Billy and John clicked on all cylinders and helped give the Bruins a chance to win. That changed late in the fourth quarter.

Three minutes were left in the game when Billy hit the ground hard. After writhing in pain for some time, he got carried off the court. The trainer said it was likely a high ankle sprain.

Burdine was up by one when Billy exited the game. They couldn't hold onto the lead without him.

> *And that will do it folks. The Bruins fall to the Pikeville Pirates yet again, with the final score being eighty-two to seventy-six. I hope everyone has a Happy Halloween, and I remind you all to be safe tonight. This is Carl Ables, and I thank you for listening to 97.1 The Bruin.*

John and Rachel helped Billy wobble out of the gym. Cassie walked behind them, carrying Billy's gym bag. Shane hopped out of his car and opened the back door.

"Well, this definitely throws a wrench in our plan for tonight," John said, easing Billy into the back seat. "We need to regroup and adjust the strategy since Billy can barely walk."

"It's already dark, so we probably can't get to The Roost safely." Cassie handed Billy his bag. "Let's meet at my house. Mom is working again."

"Sounds good." Billy tossed John the keys to The Fury.

"We'll meet you over there," John said.

Rachel watched John walk toward The Fury and grabbed Cassie's wrist. "Want me to ride with y'all?"

"Thanks, but I'll be fine." Cassie closed the door to Shane's car and ran to catch up with John.

***

"We can't call it off, Jimmy. It has to be tonight." Darrell spoke with confidence. "It's the darkest night of the year, the best night to figure out what we're dealing with."

"Halloween night, the darkest night of the year," Jimmy mumbled. "Great time to wander in the woods after a witch."

Shane looked out the front window, where the darkness was already heavy. "What if the witch already visited her coven and left?"

"From my studies, the witch waits until the moon is at its highest point in the sky before returning to its coven. So," Darrell insisted, "the witch will be there at midnight at the earliest."

John raised his wrist so the others could see the face of his watch. It read eight o'clock.

"Alright, so what's the plan?" Billy lay back on the couch with his ankle propped up in Rachel's lap.

"We go on with the plan," John said. "Shane, Jimmy, and Darrell—you guys will be in the boat. You got it stryx-proof, right?"

Shane nodded. "Just like T.O.A.S.T, but on the water. Garlic-painted enclosure, cross windows, wooden stakes, and a lantern hanging off the front."

"Cassie, Rachel"—John pointed at the two girls—"you'll be in the car at the boat ramp, with the boat trailer in the water, waiting for extraction. If you get into any trouble, drive away, no exceptions."

"Any trouble, we're outta there," Rachel promised.

"There's only one change to the plan." John nodded toward Billy. "He'll be with you in the car."

"No way!" Billy started to swing his legs off the couch, but a piercing pain put an end to that. He gritted his teeth until the pain subsided. "You aren't hiking to the coven alone."

"I'll be fine," John said. "Nothing will be able to see me once I'm down in the foxhole."

"Foxhole?" Darrell asked.

John explained that he and Shane spent the past week digging a trench near the coven. They placed a little roof of branches over the top to hide under. Then they covered the roof leaves with garlic.

"It's safe," John told Darrell.

"I don't care how safe it is," Billy said, "you're not going by yourself."

"I'll go with him!"

"Absolutely not, Cassie." A surge of adrenaline ran through John's veins, and he faintly heard Cassie's heart speed up. "There's no way I'm going to let you hike forty-five minutes up the mountain alongside a creek in the dark when those vampire bats are out and about."

Cassie's neck and face turned bright red. "There is no way you're doing that alone. Especially with that big stryx stalking your every move."

John threw his hands in the air. "That's exactly why you can't go with me!"

Cassie crossed her arms. "We don't have time to argue. I'm going with you, and that's final."

John looked to Billy for support, but Billy was suddenly fascinated with the couch upholstery.

"Fine, whatever." John slung his backpack over his shoulder. "But we got to go now."

***

Billy and Rachel sat in the car as the others boated across the lake, cutting through dense fog that hugged the water's surface. The fog seemed to silence the area. The only noises heard were cool gusts of wind drifting across the lake, the slap of the waves crashing against the boat, and the occasional distant screech.

Cramped inside the makeshift boat cabin made out of scrap metal and wooden planks, the group stared out the small cross-shaped window.

"Alright, John," Jimmy whispered, "run through your supplies."

John opened his bookbag and held up each item, one at a time. Hand flares. Flare gun. Binoculars. Glow sticks. B batteries for the flashlight. Canteen of water. Coffee beans to chew on, in case he got tired. A few random snacks.

Jimmy gave a thumbs up.

Shane pointed to the front of the boat. "Alright guys, we're approaching the drop off."

John reached down and tightened the calf holster that held wooden stakes.

"Remember," Darrell said, "once you see it, the mission is complete. Get out of there as quick as possible. If you don't see the witch by three a.m., assume you're not going to."

John nodded.

"Oh, one last thing." Darrell leaned close to ensure John heard him. "If you do see the witch—"

Something lighted on top of the boat. Cassie, John, Darrell, and Shane froze in terror and stared up at the makeshift boat roof, the only thing separating them from the stryx. They listened as the creature took a step toward the back of the boat and then pushed off into the night.

John exhaled and glanced at his watch: ten twenty-eight. He turned to Cassie and whispered, "Last chance to stay here."

Cassie shook her head.

"Well," John said, "let's get a move on then."

***

John and Cassie hiked alongside the creek bank,

using the rushing stream for navigation and smothering their conversation.

"You okay?" John asked.

Cassie nodded. "Just ready to be in the foxhole and not out in the open."

The pair continued wandering through the dark until John squatted down. He pulled his bag off his shoulders and pulled out a glow stick, then cracked it. "Alright," he said, "we're moving away from the creek now, so we have to be much quieter. Stay close."

Cassie held the back of John's hoodie as they ventured into the forest. Singing crickets replaced the sound of rushing water, and the orange glow stick provided just enough visibility to see the next step. They crept forward slowly, working their way around low branches and briars. Eventually, the foxhole came into view.

"There it is," John said. "Come on."

He took a confident step forward and—*SNAP!*—stepped on a twig.

A petrifying screech shook the leaves on the trees around them. John pulled Cassie's hand toward the hole, and the two jumped inside. John yanked the roof over their heads and stuffed the glow stick under his hoodie.

Minutes passed, and the woods quieted again. John peeked through a small opening in the leafy roof. "Part three is complete," he said into the walkie-talkie. "We have made it to the foxhole. Going radio silent now."

Billy responded with a quick "Ten-four."

"Copy," Shane replied. "We're here if you need us."

John closed the walkie and looked at his watch. Eleven twenty—forty minutes until go time.

Cassie sidled up to John to help watch for the witch.

"Here" John whispered, handing a small candy bar to Cassie.

Cassie opened her mouth wide. "Aw, a Zagnut? That's my favorite!"

"Happy Halloween."

***

John dropped the bag of coffee beans into his backpack. He didn't need them. His old nocturnal ways were returning, and he couldn't sleep if he wanted to. His watch read two twenty-five, and there was no sign of the witch. John shifted to get a better look at Cassie, as she snoozed quietly on his shoulder. The small movement caused Cassie to stir awake.

John grinned. "Good morning."

Cassie wiped drool from her mouth and popped a couple coffee beans into her mouth.

"It was nice to have you fall asleep on me again," John said.

"Oh, was it?"

"I was busy while you slept." John squinted out of the foxhole at the coven. "I imagined telling you all the things I've wanted to say these past few weeks."

Cassie yawned. "Well, stop imagining," she said quietly. "I'm awake now."

John said, "Sorry for not telling you about your dad."

"Jimmy told me that he begged you not to say anything," Cassie said. "He said you two got into a pretty heated argument over it."

John lowered his head. "I should've told you though."

Cassie touched John's arm. "Is that all you imagined yourself saying?"

"No."

"Well, come on," she said, tugging on his hoodie sleeve. "I want to hear."

Just as John was about to spill his guts, leaves crunched outside. Someone—something was walking. John and Cassie held their breath and watched a pair of dark feet shuffle by. This was followed by a clinking and rattling that grew louder and louder. Then Cassie gasped. John pulled Cassie against his chest and covered her mouth with his hand, stifling her whimper.

Cassie fought to catch her breath, as a pair of lifeless eyes stared into the foxhole. Another quick rattling sound. The eyes and the body they were attached to scooted away along the ground. The witch dragged the mangled corpse toward the coven.

John removed his hand from Cassie's mouth as soon as the witch closed the coven door.

"I'm scared," Cassie cried.

John squeezed her hands. "We're going to be okay."

They crawled out of the foxhole and tiptoed away from the coven and toward the creek.

"Yo, guys, come in! It's three o'clock. See anything? Are y'all okay?"

"What are you doing, Shane?" John flung his backpack to the ground and dug through it to find the walkie-talkie. He turned it off, but it was too late. A stryx dropped through the trees and landed in front of the creek. John flipped on his flashlight and pointed it at the

     Brock Enloe

creature. A scar spanned the thing's face.

John handed a hand flare to Cassie. "Take this, and get back to the boat."

"Wait, what?"

But John didn't answer. He sprinted into the forest, followed by the scarred stryx.

# CHAPTER 16

# MYRTU-CURIER

John's heart pounded louder than his feet on the leaf-covered forest floor. He dropped under a willow tree and scoped out the forest. The boat's lantern glowed in the distance. John counted to twenty. There was no movement nearby, so he jogged along the creek until he heard a high-pitched scream. He dropped to the ground and waited. Another scream came shortly. It was human.

"Cassie!" John grabbed the flare gun and bolted back into the woods toward the direction of the scream. Breaking branches and stumbling over tree roots, he trampled through the dark, yelling for Cassie. When he emerged into a small clearing, he saw her. She was on her back, surrounded by strigoi.

He raised the flare gun and fired into the air, causing the strigoi to scurry away. Cassie was bloodied and bruised, but she wasn't bitten. John dragged her to her feet and rushed toward the boat.

The stalking stryx screeched overhead. John turned toward the creek. "We can't put the others at risk!" he cried.

Holding hands, Cassie and John jumped from rock to rock across the creek, as the screeching grew nearer.

"I can't run anymore," Cassie said.

John threw her onto his back and pushed forward. Using the canopy of trees as cover, he continued to run until he reached the edge of the wood line. A wide field spread out before them. John set Cassie down.

"There." Cassie pointed. "We'll be safe there."

A wooden barn stood two hundred yards away, in the middle of the field.

"We'd never make it," John said. "That stryx would be on us before we even get halfway."

"We can't stay here," Cassie said. "We can't."

John surveyed the area. A craggy cliffside reached up to the mountain's peak, and an old country road was in the distance. Accessing either left them exposed for way too long.

"So, what do you think?" Cassie asked.

"I think that barn is our only hope."

Darting across the barren field, they raced against the sound of wings, doing their best to outpace the pursuing beast. The stryx screamed in anger, pumping its wings ferociously. Fifty yards from the barn, the thing dove and knocked John to the ground.

"John!"

"Run, Cassie! Get to the barn!" John pulled a wooden stake from his calf holster and stared down the scar-faced monster. "Come on!" he screamed.

He lunged at the stryx, and the beast dug its talons into John's side and flung him into the air. John slammed against the ground, blood trickling down his face. The stryx reared back both claws and suddenly turned away. With a snarl, the thing grabbed Cassie from its back and threw her to the ground.

"Cassie!" John got to his feet and thrust the wooden stake into the stryx's heart. The beast screeched and collapsed.

Cassie hurried to John and draped his arm over her back. She helped him limp to the barn, as distant screeches grew closer. She slammed the barn door shut and locked it, then propped John up on a pile of hay. A lantern hung on a nearby stall door. Cassie struck up the hand flare and used it to light the lantern.

"Here, let me help you." She slowly pulled the slashed hoodie and t-shirt from John's body.

Deep claw marks stretched across his chest. Cassie wet John's shirt with water from the canteen.

"You saved me," she uttered as she dabbed blood from John's brow.

"I think you got it backwards," John said. "You saved me."

"Why'd you do it?" Cassie poured more water on the shirt. "You risked your life for me."

John grimaced as Cassie wiped a cut on his shoulder. "I did it because..." He clenched his fists and forced himself to stay still while Cassie cleaned his wounds. "I love you. And there's nothing you can say or do that will ever make me stop loving you."

Cassie traced the contours of John's jaw with her

     Brock Enloe

hand and leaned in. John followed suit, and then their lips met.

"I love you." Cassie crawled into John's lap and ran her hands through his sweaty hair. They kissed until Cassie brushed up against one of John's cuts, causing him to flinch. Cassie got off his lap and apologized.

"It's okay," John said. "Really, I'm fine."

Cassie crawled to John's side and looked at his watch. "Three hours until sunrise."

***

"Rough night?" The waitress at Breakfast & Stuff dropped menus on the table.

John considered his ripped, bloody clothing. "Yeah, you could say that."

The waitress took their orders with a cocked eyebrow and walked away.

John lowered his head and put both hands on the table. "Well, we saw the witch."

Darrell's eyes widened.

"Okay, so that means what?" Shane looked at Darrell. "Which witch is which?"

"We're dealing with the death witch," Darrell mumbled.

Jimmy rubbed his arms. "Of course we are."

"But that's not all we saw," Cassie chimed in.

"There's more?" Jimmy asked.

John tapped his thumbs against the table. "The witch drug this dead body right in front of the foxhole. I mean, it's eyes literally stared at us."

"Did you recognize the body?" Billy asked.

"No, no clue who it was," Cassie said, "but that poor person was dead."

Darrell said something to himself.

"What?" Rachel asked.

"That was her victim, the reason the witch was there to begin with." Darrell continued, "In order to retain her power and strength, the witch has to feed on the night of the Stygian moon."

John felt a tingling sensation in his neck. "You didn't think to tell us that detail before we left?"

"I tried to, but then that stryx landed on the boat."

"Speaking of," Cassie said, "John killed the big stryx that was stalking him."

***

Several weeks passed with little progress. Since Darrell was the least familiar with the Myrtu-curier, everyone had to dig up any information they could find on the death witch.

Darrell and Shane found a book at the public library with two crucial bits of information.

Salt can hurt a witch and prevent it from coming near.

Burning incense at night near a witch's domain can attract a witch.

Upon learning this, Darrell lined the perimeter of The Roost with salt. He also recommended surveillance to learn the witch's habits, patterns, and characteristics. So, someone from the group headed to the state park every

        Brock Enloe

night with a handful of incense and a pair of binoculars. Within twenty minutes, the witch always appeared. While this provided some information about the witch, it didn't help them know how to properly kill it.

Someone knocked on John's bedroom door and walked in. It was Cassie. "Shane radioed like fifteen minutes ago. He wants us at The Roost."

John jumped off his bed and slid on his shoes.

"Shane said something about Darrell knowing how to kill the witch," Cassie said as they speedwalked toward The Roost.

"Billy can't—"

"We know," Cassie said. "He's doing dinner with those college recruits. But Shane said this can't wait."

When they entered The Roost, Shane motioned for Cassie and John to have a seat. "Darrell thinks he's onto something."

Darrell had been researching the death witch and called all the local libraries to see if they had any books about witch species. The library on the other side of Newburg had a book, and it sounded promising. There was just one issue. The library closed in an hour and a half, and it would take an hour to get there.

John screwed up his face. "So what are we waiting for? Cassie and I will go with you."

Darrell waved a finger at John. "No, I need you, Cassie, and Jimmy to watch the witch one more time. Me and Shane will get the book. Hopefully," Darrell said, "that will get us all the info we need to do away with the witch."

# CHAPTER 17

# THE LAST PATROL

"Dude, it's freezing!" John sat in back seat of Mrs. Bardot's station wagon, blowing into his hands.

"This ain't nothing," Jimmy said. "Just wait until December and January roll around."

"There is literally snow on the ground," John said. "What do you mean this is nothing?"

Cassie turned in her seat to look at John. "It's maybe two inches of snow. This mid-November snow is just a warm up."

"Okay, okay, I get it. But y'all forget," John said, "I'm not from here. I'm not used to snow."

Jimmy laughed and passed a slice of pizza to John. "Eat that," he said. "It'll warm you up."

"You think the witch will show?" Cassie said.

John chewed thoughtfully. "She has every other time we've done this."

"Won't she see us?" Jimmy asked.

"See us? No. But she may hear us if you keep smacking that loud," John joked.

Another uneventful half hour passed with no sign of the witch.

Cassie set the binoculars in her lap. "Has it ever taken this long?"

"Something's up," John said. "Hand me those."

Cassie gave the binoculars to John. He looked across the field at the incense sticks.

"Shoot," John said. "Incense is out. I got to go relight it."

"Dude, are you crazy?" Jimmy said. "You can't go out there. What if it's a trap?"

Cassie agreed and suggested they head home.

"Darrell told us to learn the witch's habits." John looked through the binoculars. "It was probably just snow that fell from the tree branches and put out the incense."

Jimmy pleaded with John to stay in the car.

"How about this," John said. "You stay put, and I'll be right back."

A rush of cold air came into the car as John opened the back door and stepped into the night. Snow crunched under his feet as he crept toward the incense pile in the distance. Moonlight glistened off the snow, painting the night a warm hue of blue.

Cassie watched through the binoculars as John shuffled forward, fighting through the snow flurries dancing around his face.

John reached the incense pile and squatted. There wasn't a flake of snow touching the incense. He looked around frantically, then relaxed. "Must have been the wind," he said under his breath. He added a few stones around the incense to protect against the wind and wiggled the lighter out of his pocket. His numb fingers struggled to produce a flame from the lighter.

"Come on, come on, come on."

Something rustled behind the wood line. John dropped the lighter and leapt behind the nearest tree.

Cassie held the binoculars against her face and reached for Jimmy. "Something's wrong."

"Wait, what?" Jimmy dropped his pizza. "What's going on?"

"Look!"

Jimmy grabbed the binoculars. "She's there! She baited him in!"

The witch released a spine-chilling cackle. John closed his eyes and worked to calm his breathing.

"She sees him," Jimmy whispered. "His breathing—it's too cold out there. She sees his breathing."

As the witch approached the tree, John reached into his pocket. The witch moved slowly toward him, her raspy breathing sending shivers up John's spine. She cackled again, and John pressed his back against the tree, clutching a fistful of salt.

All of a sudden, a harsh honk rang through the forest.

"What did you do?" Jimmy said.

Cassie dropped her hands from the steering wheel, as the witch's head snapped toward The Fury.

"Oh, Cassie," Jimmy said, "we are so screwed."

Cassie slammed her hand against the horn again, then opened her door and shouted, "RUN!"

John took off for The Fury, his efforts slowed by the fresh snow. As he raced, the sound of crunching snow behind him grew louder and closer. He pumped his arms to run faster, then stepped on a small sheet of ice. The fall to the ground was fast, and the witch was even faster. In an instant, the wretched witch stood over John, cackling and showing off her sharp, jagged teeth.

John panted as he took in her pointy crinkled nose, stringy hair, and pockmarked skin. When he looked into her black eyes, he froze, trance-like.

"Move!" Jimmy shouted.

John shook his head, flung the salt into the witch's face, and rolled to the left as Jimmy floored the old station wagon and ran into the witch. The witch tumbled backward and let out an unnatural groan.

John slipped and slid his way into the car. "Punch it!"

Jimmy obeyed, and the tires spun uselessly in the snow. A cloud of grey exhaust filled the air.

"We're stuck!!" Cassie shouted.

John jumped back into the cold and pressed against the wagon's back bumper. "Jimmy," he yelled, "I need your help."

"She's getting up!" Jimmy shouted.

John looked up as the witch's bones snapped and popped into place. "Jimmy—come on, man, I need you!"

Cassie scooted onto the edge of the driver's seat. "Help him or we're all dead!"

Jimmy surrendered the driver's seat and rushed to help John.

"Push!" John strained against the back of the car. The veins in his neck pulsed, and the bite marks glowed. Then, the wagon broke loose and zoomed forward, slamming into the witch a second time.

***

Cassie, John, Jimmy, Billy, and Rachel sat in Cassie's living room. Outside, a car door closed and two sets of footsteps hurried to the front door.

Shane came in first, smiling. Darrell followed, holding a book in the air.

Jimmy smacked John on the arm excitedly. "They got it!"

"Does it have the information we need?" John asked.

"Does it?" Darrell smirked. "Man, this book has it all. It squawks every detail about the witch."

Shane slapped his legs. "It's time to kill a witch!"

Darrell slammed the book on his lap, starting a small dust storm. He coughed and riffled through the old pages. "Right here," he said, tapping the bottom right section of a page. "Read this."

John grabbed the book and read aloud: "In order to kill a death witch, one must pierce her heart with the talon of the beast she controls. And to ensure the witch will not return, cut her head off and burn the body before dawn."

"Keep reading."

"Beyond the part where I have to stab the witch with a stryx talon?"

"Keep reading," Darrell repeated.

John continued: "It is crucial to maintain the element of surprise. The death witch is the most feared and dangerous witch species of all. It has no regard for human life, and if it knows you are coming, you are dead already."

Jimmy looked sick to his stomach.

"So, how does this help us?" John asked.

Darrell took the book and flipped a few more pages. "If the witch knows it is being hunted," he read, "it will begin to bait and set traps for the hunters. Turning the hunters into prey, it will try to isolate them and pick them off one by one."

"Which is exactly what it did tonight," Jimmy said gloomily.

Darrell held up a hand and continued. "Once you have been discovered, the only option is to burn its coven. This will draw the witch's attention for a short time and weaken her power, though it will also greatly anger the witch. There is no guarantee this method will work, but the odds would shift in your favor slightly. With the witch's powers dampened, she will act off of emotion, not logic. She will be aggressive and attack, but she will do so without strategy or forethought, which may leave her vulnerable."

"So," John said after a long silence. "What do you guys think?"

Shane eased into the couch cushions. "You really got to ask?"

# CHAPTER 18

# HUNT FOR THE WITCH

*After we kill the witch tonight, life goes back to normal. No more dangerous missions, no more fighting vampire creatures or witches, nothing. It will all be over.*

"Okay, I'm done." John set his journal down. "Let's run through the plan one last time."

"Before we do that," Darrell said, "I'd like to say something."

John motioned for Darrell to take the floor.

Darrell stood up. "I just want to say thank you guys for making me part of the group. I know I'm a bit weird, but... Well, no matter what happens tonight, I'm happy to be here with you all."

Shane patted Darrell on the back. John insisted he wasn't weird.

"And one more thing. I made you guys something!"

Darrell opened his bag and handed out handmade toy pistols. "This is for Shane. Jimmy. Billy. Cassie and Rachel."

Billy held his up and laughed. "Thanks, dude, but a fake gun won't help us."

"They're not fake," Darrell said. "They shoot salt."

"Take that, witches!" Shane held his salt gun up in a threatening pose. "These are sick!"

Darrell dug deeper into his bag. "And for you."

John admired his custom salt gun.

"Dude," Shane said, "that looks familiar."

John turned the gun over in his hand. "It's just like Stallone's gun in *Cobra*."

"Cassie told me you were a big Stallone guy," Darrell explained. "I call it the salt sub-machine gun. That witch won't dare come near you with that thing."

"Thanks, dude!" John grabbed Darrell and hugged him, pinning his arms to his side.

"Alright guys," Billy said, "dusk is in two hours. Let's review the plan."

***

Shane and Jimmy left The Roost and headed toward the boat.

"You guys be safe." Cassie handed John his gear and kissed his cheek. "I love you."

Rachel opened the door, and the handcar rolled out of The Roost, carrying John, Billy, and Darrell.

Billy blew Rachel a kiss. "See you guys up there."

With the boys out of sight, Cassie and Rachel locked

up The Roost and headed to The Fury.

John made a final supply check as the handcar weaved through the trees.

"Is that what I think it is?" Darrell asked.

John held up a giant, discolored talon taped to a broken broom handle. "Second time that stryx attacked me, it left this behind in my shoulder."

Darrell started to comment when Cassie's voice called through the walkie-talkie: "We're in position."

"T-minus twenty minutes, and we'll be in position, too," Billy said in response. He looked at the setting sun. "Better get a move on, boys."

"We're crossing the lake now and should make it before dark," Shane said into the walkie. "We'll make contact once the fire starts."

Jimmy rocked back and forth on his seat as Shane drove the boat across the lake.

"Relax, dude, we got the easy job." Shane gave the boat more throttle. "We burn the coven, sail back across the lake, and then meet the others."

"I know, I know," Jimmy said, watching the sun setting behind the snowy mountain ahead.

"By the time we get back to the others, the witch will probably be dead."

"You're right." Jimmy blew into his hands. "I'm overthinking."

Shane eased off the throttle. "You know what'll help calm your nerves?" He grabbed a portable radio from under the seat. "Music."

The opening riff of "Don't Fear the Reaper" played over the radio's single speaker.

"Not now," Jimmy said. "I'm trying not to think about dying."

Shane laughed and scrolled the dial to the next clear station. Daryl Hall sang the monstrously upbeat "Maneater."

"Seriously?" Jimmy said.

Shane flipped through a few more stations until landing on the local rock channel. A scream from "The Last in Line" threatened to rip the small stereo's speaker in half.

"I ain't cutting this off," Shane said. "I love Dio!"

Shane cranked the volume and sang along. As they boated across the lake, Jimmy wondered if they would ever return home.

***

Half an hour after sunset, John, Billy, and Darrell sat in the handcar, waiting.

"We wait five more minutes," Billy said. "If we don't hear from them by then, we move on with the plan and hope they did their part."

The boys sat still, their legs aching to get up and out of the armored handcar when Shane cried out over the walkie.

"It got Jimmy! The coven is burning, but the witch got Jimmy, man!"

"What do you mean, it got Jimmy?" Billy yelled.

"Is he dead?" Cassie asked.

"The witch came out of nowhere, man!" Shane said.

"Where is the witch now?" Billy asked.

"I shot her with the salt gun and managed to pull Jimmy into the foxhole, but..." Shane breathed heavily into the walkie. "I lost visual."

"Guys, we've got a problem." Cassie's voice was almost inaudible over the walkie-talkie. "The witch is here."

"Cassie, stay put!" John called into the walkie. "I'm on the way!"

John tightened his calf holster and adjusted the small flashlight on his salt gun. "Change of plans," he said, handing the stryx spear to Darrell. "You're going to drive this into the witch. I've got to go."

Darrell held the spear. "But what are you doing?"

"Me?" John said, exiting the handcar. "I'm the bait."

Billy watched his little brother vanish into the woods, then yelled back into the walkie. "Shane, get Jimmy to the hospital now. Don't bother meeting back up with us. Get to the boat and get Jimmy help. Don't let him die!"

"Ten-four," Shane said. "Godspeed!"

Billy dropped the walkie into his bag and slapped Darrell on the chest. "Showtime!"

The two of them leapt out of the handcar and headed toward the ranger's hut. Behind them, John hurdled fallen trees and pushed through clumps of snow, his small flashlight cutting through the darkness as strigoi screeches grew to a crescendo.

At a small opening, John spotted an unlit pile of incense sitting in the middle of a field. The Fury sat in the parking lot nearby. John scurried to the incense and lit it, then hustled across the field to check on the girls. The car doors hung open. John's heart sank. The girls were gone.

He raised his salt gun and covered the car in dim light

from his flashlight. Walking around The Fury, he spotted three sets of footprints and several drops of blood leading into the woods. John swallowed hard and followed the blood trail until it ran out.

"What the?"

John spun around, desperately trying to locate more blood or footprints. But there were none. He slowly lifted his flashlight to regain his bearings when a stryx pounced on top of him and pinned him to the ground. John flailed helplessly on his back, staring up at the beast's saliva that dripped onto his face. He reached down toward his calf, but the stakes were out of reach.

The creature lowered its head and opened its mouth as a loud squeal echoed through the trees.

"Cassie?" John clenched his fists and felt his fangs push out of his mouth and against his lips. Using every ounce of energy, he raised his legs and he flipped over backward, kicking the beast away in the process.

Back on his feet, John slipped a wooden stake from his holster and beckoned the stryx to charge. The stryx obliged, leaping forward. It knocked John's stake away furiously before crumpling to the ground.

"Billy!" John shouted. "Where'd you come from?"

Billy yanked a stake out of the stryx's back. "Suck on that, you leech!"

Darrell dropped to his knees and ripped open Billy's bag. "The girls!"

Billy grabbed the walkie-talkie from his bag. "Rachel, Cassie—come in!"

Through the walkie's static, Cassie's trembling voice emerged. "It's in here with us."

"Where are you?" Billy begged.

"The ranger's hut."

***

"Salt guns out." John nudged the door to the ranger's hut open.

"Nothing in here," Billy said. "Check the back left wing, and I'll go—"

"Wait," Darrell interrupted, "do you guys hear that?"

Something scraped against a wall. The trio wandered into the left wing, following the sound. When they turned a corner, their flashlights fell on a familiar arm. The witch tilted her head and cackled, then began crawling toward them at supernatural speed.

"Shoot it!" John yelled.

The witch shrieked as the boys battered her with salt and charged past them, swatting John out of the way as she bolted through the ranger's hut and out into the forest.

"Cassie? Rachel?" John staggered to his feet and rushed down the hall, wiping blood from his forehead.

"In here!"

John pushed open a heavy door and found Cassie holding Rachel in her lap. Rachel's legs were covered in blood.

Billy fell to his knees and cupped Rachel's head with his hands. "What happened?"

"I'm fine," Rachel said. "It's not as bad as it looks."

"The Fury wouldn't crank, so we tried to make a run for it," Cassie said. "The witch got ahold of her leg and gashed it pretty badly. It's bleeding."

"I'm okay," Rachel squeezed Billy's hand. "I swear."

"We're done here," John said. "Jimmy may be dead for all we know and Rachel, I can't risk this anymore. I say we fight our way back to The Fury and go home."

"And just let you and Billy turn into one of those creatures?" Darrell said.

"Did you not hear me?" Cassie said calmly. "The Fury won't crank."

"Then we take the handcar down the mountain," John said.

"No!" Cassie dug her fingernails into John's arm. "We came this far. We are killing this witch tonight."

"Tonight is our best shot." Darrell turned off his flashlight. "Shane and Jimmy burned the coven. The witch is weak. If she rebuilds the coven, she'll regain her strength."

"That witch didn't look weak to me!" Billy aimed his flashlight at Rachel's wounds.

"It's now or never," Darrell said plainly. "Do or die."

# CHAPTER 19

# DO OR DIE

"Baby, breathe." Cassie looked at John, desperately trying to calm him down. "We need you. I need you. Please help us figure out a plan."

John inhaled deeply, then asked Darrell to put a salt barrier around the room. As Darrell went to work, John inspected the remaining gear. There wasn't much left, but they still had the stryx spear.

"Not ideal," John said, "but it's doable."

Billy touched his growing fangs with the tip of his tongue. "What're you thinking?"

"The book said that the witch will reverse roles if it knows it's being hunted. Isn't that right, Darrell?" John said. "Won't the witch become the hunter?"

"Yeah, so what?"

"So we play into that," John said. "We walk into the witch's trap, and we reverse the roles again."

Darrell put the final touches on the salt barrier.

"We become the bait," he said, "in order to become the hunter."

"Exactly!" John remarks.

"I still don't follow," Billy admitted.

"The witch knows we're trapped in here. She expects us to make a run for The Fury eventually, so she's probably out there somewhere, waiting for us. So, give her what she wants—we take the bait and make a dash for the car." John's eyes light up. "But what the witch doesn't know is that we want her to follow us."

"Then what?" Rachel asked.

"Then we reverse the roles," John said, "and kill her."

***

John held Cassie's hand and moved quietly toward The Fury through the biting November air.

"Something is bothering you," Cassie said. "What is it?"

A wisp of cold air floated out and away from John's mouth. "I shouldn't have sent Jimmy to the coven."

"He wanted to help. It was his choice. Plus," Cassie said, "I'm sure he's at the hospital by now and everything is fine."

With no sign of the witch, they forged ahead to The Fury. John popped the hood as Cassie dropped salt in a perimeter around the car.

"Remember," John said, "not all the way around."

Cassie nodded, as John updated to the others on the walkie-talkie. Fifteen minutes later, John opened the driver's door and stepped out.

"Close the hood so I can see you," Cassie said, "and be careful."

John slammed the hood with a satisfying thud, only to look into Cassie's wide eyes.

"John!"

Before John could turn, the witch smacked him to the ground, knocking the breath out of him. Cassie looked toward the woods, where the others were supposed to be stationed. She dropped into The Fury's floorboard. "Where are you guys?" she called into the walkie-talkie. "The witch is here. Close the salt barrier!"

Static screamed back through the walkie.

"Guys!" Cassie yelled. "We're out of salt, and the witch is in position. Close the barrier!"

"Abort!" Billy said into the walkie. "A stryx—we're pinned down. Abort!"

Cassie took three slow breaths, then cracked open the passenger's door to help John. Something slammed against the front windshield. Cassie looked up. John's face pressed against the glass.

"Stay in the car!" he shouted, as the witch slashed at his back. Blood spewed out of his back and ran down the window. He cried out in pain, then rolled off the hood and out of view.

Cassie kicked the passenger door open and got backhanded by the witch. John climbed to his feet and grabbed the stryx spear from his back. As he did, the handle fell to the hard snow, leaving John with a spear no longer than a dagger.

John palmed the shortened weapon and shrugged. "Hey, witch!" He popped the witch with a salt pellet.

        Brock Enloe

The witch's head snapped in his direction. Her beady black eyes bore into John.

"Come on, you crone." John tossed the salt gun to the side and gripped the shortened spear.

"John, no!" Cassie closed her eyes.

John gritted his teeth and dug his feet into the ground. Just when the witch was close enough to strike, a car engine revved up. John stumbled backward as the car pinned the witch against a tree.

Smoke poured out from under the station wagon's hood. The driver's door popped open, and Shane tumbled out.

"What are you waiting for?" he said. "Kill her!"

John raised the stryx talon and plunged it into the witch's chest. The witch shrieked in agony and quivered dramatically. She reached her withered hand toward John and spat, then bowed her head.

Darrell, Rachel, and Billy limped out of the woods and stared at the witch's limp body.

"Is she dead?" Rachel asked.

John closed his eyes and said, "Yes."

Billy rushed to John's side. "It's over, man. It's over!"

"Not quite." Darrell handed Billy an axe. "There's one more thing to do."

***

John, Cassie, Rachel, Billy, Darrell, and Shane looked on as embers from the beheaded witch's burning body mingled with morning sunbeams peeking over the mountain.

"Shane, you're dead."

Shane flicked dirt off his pants. "Why you say that, Billy?"

"You ruined that car. Jimmy's mom is going to kill you."

Shane laughed nervously.

"Hey," John said, "how is Jimmy?"

"He's not looking good." Shane picked up a small handful of snow and tossed it aimlessly. "Doc said he probably wouldn't make it to lunch…"

John's eyes filled with tears. Rachel whimpered.

"Then again," Shane continued, "he never looked that good."

Cassie scrunched her face.

"And he won't make it to lunch," Shane said, "not without a big breakfast."

"Wait," Billy said, "he won't—what's going on?"

Shane grinned and threw a small snowball at Billy. "Jimmy's fine. Well, he's going to be fine."

"Dude seriously?" John wiped his eyes.

Billy punched Shane on the arm. "Not cool!"

# CHAPTER 20

# BACK TO NORMAL

"Get the net!" John pulled back hard on his fly rod.

Jimmy ran toward John and nearly fell into the lake.

"Get it!" John said.

Jimmy dipped the net into the water and pulled out a writhing brown trout.

"This thing is huge!" Jimmy said. "At least twenty-two inches."

"Dude, let's go!" John reached for the fish with both hands. "That's my PR!" He held the fish a moment, then released it back into the cold, flowing water.

Jimmy sighed as the fish swam away.

"Aren't you glad we skipped school now?" John asked.

Jimmy strapped the net to his waist and cast in the direction where the big brown disappeared. "So," he said, "you ask Cassie to the Bearhug Ball yet?"

John watched his line float in the water. "No, not yet. I don't know how to ask her."

"You just say, 'Hey Cassie, would you like to go to the dance with me?' It's that simple." Jimmy let some line out.

"If it's that simple, have you asked Bridget yet?" John said.

"You mean Brenda?" Jimmy chuckled. "And yes, I have asked her."

"Really?" John whipped his line backward, then forward and let it drop to the water. "What did she say?"

"What do you think she said?" Jimmy said confidently. "Look at me! I'm a hunk!"

John grinned. "Good for you, man."

"I told Brenda we were being chauffeured on the handcar," Jimmy said, "so you better not flake, and you better ask Cassie soon."

"Sheesh, calm down, Mr. Chunk!"

"It's Mr. Hunk, my friend."

John promised that he would ask Cassie that night while they were on their date. Then he glanced at his watch. It was already four thirty.

"Oh shoot," he said, "we gotta go now!"

***

John opened the passenger door of The Fury and bowed. "So sorry I'm late, Cassie. Hopefully we won't lose our reservation."

"Reservations, huh?" Cassie felt her heart race.

John pulled out of her driveway and sped away. When they cruised into the steak house parking lot, Cassie fought back tears.

"Your mom said that your dad brought you here when you guys had something to celebrate."

A tear rolled down Cassie's cheek. "What big event are we celebrating tonight?"

"How about you come inside and find out?" John wiped Cassie's cheek, then went around The Fury to open her door.

Inside the restaurant, Cassie watched red and orange flames dance in the oversized fireplace. "This is perfect."

"I'm glad you think so." John glanced around the dim room before reaching across the table to hold her hand.

"So, you never answered my question," Cassie said, batting her eyes. "What are we celebrating?"

"For one, that our vampire bat creature-hunting days are over."

Cassie took a drink of her water. "Our witch-hunting days are over, too."

"That's right." John shook his head. "Definitely glad those days are behind us."

"So, is that all we're celebrating tonight?"

"Well, I was hoping that, uh..."

"Good evening."

John and Cassie looked up. A well-dressed waiter took a seat beside John and asked if they were ready to order or if they needed a few minutes. Cassie looked at John with confusion. John shrugged, dropped his hands to his lap, grabbed something from the waiter under the table, and said they needed to study the menu for a minute or two.

When the waiter left, John flipped through the menu with one hand. Cassie put a hand on top of John's menu and pushed it to the table.

"You were saying?"

"What was I saying?" John scooted back in his chair and rubbed his chin. "Ah yes, I was saying that I hoped we could celebrate something else tonight, but I have to ask you something first."

Cassie gave a look of playful exasperation.

"I was wanting to know if you would like to go to the Fur Ball with me?" John pulled out a bouquet of red roses from under the table.

Cassie chuckled, "You mean the Bearhug Ball?"

John looked down to hide his embarrassment.

Cassie grinned from ear to ear and pulled the roses to her nose. "I'd love to go to the Fur Ball with you, John Daggon."

"Oh, give me a break." John leaned back in his seat, the firelight dancing on his human features. "I was nervous, okay?"

"I've never seen you like this," Cassie said.

"Like what?"

"So...happy."

***

The past few months have been weird. After killing the witch, I thought things would go back to how they were before. I guess I just thought that we would wake up the next day and forget that it all happened.

I wanted to forget, to go back to being a normal teenager. But it didn't work that way, at least not for me.

                    Brock Enloe

Of course, I'm happy we broke the curse. The group hangs out almost every weekend at The Roost, but—I don't know, it's hard to explain. I didn't notice it at first. I guess we were so busy with the holidays. I mean, Thanksgiving was a few days after we killed the witch. We all had family gatherings, then we met up at The Roost for our first annual Thanksgiving, friends only. Friendsgiving? Hm—I like the sound of that. Anyway, Billy and I deep-fried a turkey, Jimmy and Shane fixed the sides, and Darrell brought drinks. Cassie and Rachel made dessert. It was magical, the best Thanksgiving ever.

At Christmas, we got pizza and exchanged gifts. Mom made cookies for us up at the house and let everyone stay over. That was quite a night!

Then New Year's. We stayed at The Roost and just had a chill night. No fireworks or anything. We'd already had our fair share of bright lights and loud explosions.

After all of that, I started to notice that I could never fully relax or let my guard down. It was frustrating, because everyone else seemed okay. They all moved on. For a while, I took it upon myself to keep an eye out. Not just for my sake or Cassie's sake, but for everyone's.

Then the past month or so, Jimmy started grilling me about the Valentine's dance at school and why I hadn't asked Cassie to be my date yet. I avoided it for as long as I could. I was so worried that if I let my guard down, the witch would return or something. I know it sounds crazy. Well, Jimmy's badgering got to me, and I eventually got over my fear of a dead witch and asked Cassie to the Bearhug Ball. Thanks to Jimmy, I stopped looking over my shoulder in fear and started looking ahead at what's actually in front of me.

I'm so glad I did, because Friday night was one of the best nights of my life. Cassie looked stunning. I'll always have an image of how she looked engraved in my brain because—wow! She wore a baby blue dress that made her eyes pop. Her curly hair was just right, and her lips looked so kissable. And they were kissable. Trust me, I kissed them—a lot. When I thought the night couldn't get any better, the DJ played our favorite bands: The Outfield, the Police, Scorpions, Poison, Bryan Adams, and we danced until they kicked us out.

Then we took the handcar back to The Roost. Me, Cassie, Jimmy, and Brenda. When we got there, Shane and his girl were there, along with Billy and Rachel. Darrell was there, too, with his dance date, Tiffany Malardson. It was legitimately the perfect night.

But enough about Friday night. I'm writing to remember what we went through this year. I write to remember the struggles we overcame. Like my grandma once said, "I write to relive the moments that have built the person I am

       Brock Enloe

today." So, here's to a year I'll never forget, the year I was a bat among bruins.

"Come on, boys! Got to eat quick or we'll be late for church."

John rushed to the kitchen table and took a seat beside Billy.

"I am so proud of you boys," Mrs. Daggon said. "You guys played great last night!"

"Thanks, Mom," John mumbled with a mouth full of food.

Dad straightened his tie as he entered the kitchen. "You brought Burdine their very first title. But then you missed the team picture." Mr. Daggon kissed his wife's cheek and tossed the day's *Burdine Post* on the table. "You guys too cool for pictures?"

John grabbed the newspaper and stared in wide-mouthed amazement. His teammates smiled behind the championship trophy that floated in air, as if suspended by unseen forces.

Billy spewed orange juice out of his mouth.

"Not again!" John ran to his room and grabbed the walkie. "Guys, we've got a problem! Guys, come in!"


THE END